BELLY OF THE WHALE

BELLY OF THE WHALE

A NOVEL

LINDA MERLINO

KÜNATI

LARGO, USA

BELLY OF THE WHALE

For information, contact Kunati Inc., Book Publishers in both USA and Canada.
In USA: 6901 Bryan Dairy Road, Suite 150, Largo, FL 33777 USA
In Canada: 75 First Street, Suite 128, Orangeville, ON L9W 5B6 CANADA,
or e-mail to info@kunati.com.

FIRST EDITION

Designed by Kam Wai Yu
Persona Corp. | www.personaco.com

ISBN-13: 978-1-60164-018-5   EAN 9781601640185
FIC000000 FICTION/General

Published by Kunati Inc. (USA) and Kunati Inc. (Canada).
Provocative. Bold. Controversial.™

http://www.kunati.com

TM—Kunati and Kunati Trailer are trademarks
owned by Kunati Inc. Persona is a trademark owned by Persona Corp.
All other trademarks are the property of their respective owners.

Library of Congress Cataloging-in-Publication Data

Merlino, Linda.
  Belly of the whale : a novel / Linda Merlino. -- 1st ed.
    p. cm.
  Summary: "A too-real fictional account of a teacher and mother who is a terminal cancer patient and has stopped all treatment but who decides to fight back when an ex-student Buddy Baker threatens her life"--Provided by publisher.
  ISBN 978-1-60164-018-5 (hardcover : alk. paper)
  1. Cancer--Patients--Fiction. 2. Murderers--Fiction. 3. Convenience stores--Fiction. I. Title.
  PS3613.E7568B46 2008
  813'.6--dc22

2008000914

D e d i c a t i o n

To my children, Justin, Genna and Caite

Acknowledgements

This book is also dedicated to my mother, Doris Rose, a breast cancer survivor and to all who have lived, died, and shared in the heartbreak of this disease.

Thank you with deep affection to my early manuscript readers: Barbara Leone, Sandra Silverio, Susan Leonard, Kymberlee Castillo, Eileen Hackett and Jack Schmidt. Your wisdom and encouragement have been my guides. Gratitude is also extended to the writers of RWG and the 92nd Street Y, and much appreciation goes out to the women of PEO and Gina Panettieri of Talcott Notch Literary Services.

To Derek Armstrong, Kam Wai Yu and James McKinnon thanks for being the best. The Kunati Three are all about making dreams come true.

...then Jonah prayed unto his God
out from the fish's belly; out of the
belly of the whale.

Jon 2:1-2

PART I

To give up hope is to give up life.

oNE

I must have passed out, because I don't remember who put me on this gurney without a blanket. There are sirens screeching, doors opening and closing, and the thunder of running feet in heavy boots. Someone wheeled me against a glass window where the cold and snow pound along its polished seams and frozen surface. My mind is lukewarm but the rest of me could freeze to death, and my head won't turn, but I know I'm not alone. I fear that the dead are gathered here in this corner of Whales Market, that the sums of several lives are laid out on gurneys like me, and that yesterday I thought the worst thing happening was my breast cancer.

Could I be dead? Has someone pronounced me dearly departed? Perhaps a coroner with a New Hampshire quarry for brains has gone to get a tag to tie on my toe. People make mistakes; even trained personnel can overlook a faint pulse or the almost indiscernible beat of a heart. The last twenty-four hours have been too significant, too necessary for story telling, to be lost in death. My legs are stiff, neither one will move, but I am breathing, I can tell anyone who is willing to listen who I am and what happened last night at Whales Market.

My name is Hudson—no, not the river in New York State— the car. I was named after a 1955 Hudson Jet, one of the last of its kind to roll off the line in Detroit, and later owned by my father, Victor Catalina. No, not the automobile; Catalina like the island off the coast of California, the place my paternal grandfather had marked as his destination when he arrived in the United States.

Giuseppe Catillano became Joseph Catalina, thanks to Ellis Island, immigration's mistake marking forever his destination and his surname as one. The sad thing is, or maybe not, my grandfather never made it to Catalina Island, never, ever. He was sent to live with relatives on the North Shore of Boston and stayed there until the day he died.

Speaking of dying, a person could die here wedged behind this cash register. There are police cars, fire trucks, ambulances and about a hundred assorted official-looking, parka-clad men stomping around and not one giving me the time of day. The sun should be coming up soon, although you may not be able to see it because the snow is still pretty intense. A true Nor'easter of a storm blew through yesterday, and I wouldn't be freezing if that damn blizzard had blown out to sea. This is Gloucester, Massachusetts, and we don't get these kinds of snowstorms very often. The weather on Cape Ann deals its injustices in other ways, out on the ocean.

I never imagined my final resting place would be Whales Market. I never thought that my last image would be a box of microwave brownies in aisle three. Cancer was supposed to be my executioner, its effects taking me down like a poison-dart gun.

Last spring I was in the best shape. I could easily run a half-marathon, passing Whales Market and threading my way along the wharf, ending up at the Harbor. Now I can barely walk from my kitchen to the living room without stopping to sit down.

If all this is confusing, please bear with me for a while. I need to explain what has happened to me, to Willy Wu and to Ruby Desmond.

When I do that, everything will make sense.

I am a thirty-eight-year-old mother of four kids, the wife of a loving husband, and a woman who yesterday had it up to her bald head with pink ribbons and walk-a-thons. Yesterday was Tuesday. Tuesday is the day I drive to Boston Women's Hospital for chemotherapy. Five months ago, an Ivy-educated oncologist removed both of my breasts and fed them to the sharks off Ned's Landing.

Okay, that last part isn't true, but the rest is fact, and since then I have become very jaded on the subject.

Speaking of subjects, I know I'm getting off mine. I've got to start some place where it's warm and I can think without shivering.

That place is my bed.

Ten Nettles Cove is about a mile from here. That's where my bed is, my kids too, and my husband. It's yesterday morning and the sun is just coming up. A triangle of light always juts across our bed like it's the seventh day of creation every day. The light sparkles and radiates against the bed covers.

My husband, Jack, likes to spoon. You know, spooning is when one person moves up behind the other, knees lock with knee-backs, and two bodies make a concave form of love and security. Jack sometimes has to pull me from my corner of the bed, the almost-over-the-edge place that I hurl myself toward during the night. I go there more often since the cancer came, since the front of me is like the back of me, and I can't tell which end of me is top or bottom. Jack stretches out his long arms, scoops his fingers under and around my shoulders and gently reels me back toward his warm body.

Once planted in the spoon position, he talks to me in sleepy whispers. At one time he spoke through my long hair that fell tumbling over the pillowcases, soft, dark, thick strands that muffled his words. Now the pillow holds a head that is almost bare, adorned by a few scarce patches that seem stubbornly resistant to the defoliating chemicals inside me. My husband's words are an early morning chant that never changes, never deviates. Jack says the same sentence, over and over.

"Hudson like the car, Catalina like the island, Hudson Catalina,

I love you." It's a game we play, Jack and I. I don't answer him the first time, the second and sometimes even the third or fourth, because I want to hear him say Hudson Catalina, I love you, again and again. Jack knows that my playfulness has a serious center. The game is all about me, reassuring me, taking care of me, and so he is patient. Jack gives me time to process his words, his love, and his unflappable presence, as he waits between pauses for my response. There is a ritual in our dawn's talk, a knowing that each of us is there for the other, and when I've been silent long enough, Jack will kiss the nape of my neck.

Like a child who has gotten the coveted piece of candy, I close my hands around his embrace and say, "Jack like the bean stalk, Emerald like your eyes, Jack Emerald I love you back."

Except for yesterday. Yesterday morning I couldn't answer him because my body was beyond caring about life and had taken my mind and soul with it. All my reserves, I thought, had been drawn upon. Jack wiggled his tongue inside my ear. This would normally send me spinning around into his face. That whole wet tongue thing in my ear gives me the creeps, and he knows it.

"Not feeling very good this morning, honey?" Jack said.

I couldn't find my voice. Answering would take too much effort, too much energy.

"What can I do? You have to tell me, Hud, you can't go silent on me." He was so close that his imploring glanced my cheek. The only thing I could emit was a huge sob. One violent shuddering cry clamored out of my floppy-skinned body. Jack's grip tightened around me. He pressed himself closer than a simple spoon should allow.

"Okay, Hud, get some tears out. I read in one of your recovery books that you need to grieve for yourself. Give yourself permission to have your own personal pity party," he said.

"Jack …"

Words starting forming somewhere in my brain, but they were slow in coming.

"Hey." He flipped over me so that his embrace was forward instead of backward. "You missed the full moon last night. A huge snow moon if I ever saw one." Jack's face nudged mine to tilt up. "The weatherman says it's going to hit us real hard later today."

"I don't care." I said the three words and shoved my chin deeper into my chest.

"You've got Boston Women's today. We have to work something out just in case the roads get bad," he said.

"I don't need to work something out. It isn't going to snow worth a damn. Besides, I said I don't care. Just leave it like that, Jack."

I unraveled myself from his arms and legs and sat up. He lay there looking at me with that corner-of-his-mouth grin that usually makes me smile back. But this was yesterday, and yesterday I was not in the mood for his grin or his kind words or anything. I just wanted to disappear, wave a wand and poof myself into oblivion. How could I tell that to Jack? I couldn't cut the cord of his faith. Instead I found my legs, stood on the cold floor and went into the bathroom to throw up.

"Hud, are you all right?" Jack said from the other side of the bathroom door. "Let me in, please." His tone was desperate and scared.

"Go to work, Jack." I managed to answer between the dry heaves. "Just go to work."

The tears were coming, rolling over my cheeks, connecting with the mucus from my nose and washing the stinging bile off my lips and chin. His head banged on the door—thud-thud, thud-thud—a deadly pounding of frustration.

"I can't help you, Jack, I can't help myself anymore," I said. "Let me be, just let go, and let me be."

My head sank deep below the rim of the toilet. I gripped its edges until the blood drained from my hands and the skin on my fingers shone porcelain on porcelain. Faint shadows of iron and rust stains were etched along the water line. The sediment from my belly floated close to my face.

I flushed the toilet. Down, down its contents swirled, down into the dank recesses of unseen places. Take me with you, I thought, consume me in your depths, swallow me whole. But there was no chance of that. Jack's banging continued, and I wondered how much time had elapsed. I didn't know the minutes. I only knew that his agony was palpable.

"I'm going to take a shower, Jack. You get the boys ready for school, and I'll be dressed when your sister arrives."

This kind of talk was reassuring. The least I could do was tell him what he wanted to hear, not what was really coursing through my head, not that death sounded sweet and peaceful. Our children and he would be fine without me. His sister, Kathy, my best friend from high school, would take care of the children. Kathy Emerald was used to putting out other people's fires. Her knack for intervention was unmatched. She would not fail me or her brother in this calamity. No, Kathy would be a stable presence until Jack married again, as he would, I was sure. This scenario played itself out in my mind over and over. Sometimes I would even go so far as to imagine Jack and his second wife in bed together.

This disease messes you up. Your normal thinking is awash in chemicals and you go to dark places that you never knew existed inside your head.

The banging stopped, and Jack moved away from the door. I visualized him shrugging his shoulders, rubbing his forehead and resigning to my mandate.

House sounds began. The high-low voice of our thirteen-year-old son grew impatient as his younger twin brothers engaged in their morning wrestle. The boys took their cues from Jack. The thought of their mother being sick, so sick that she couldn't make dinner, wash laundry, shoot hoops or drive them to school, was avoided, denied—whatever it took not to face the truth. This morning to them was just like every other morning, and Jack's shush to be quiet carried no hint of what lay ahead. Even the whispering of some message I couldn't hear, but knew was about me, didn't alarm them.

Still on my knees, I crawled over to the tub, leaned my weight against the frigid tiles and slowly pulled myself upright. The water shot out of the showerhead, and I got within range of its outpour, clothes and all. I closed my eyes and saw the face of my four-year-old daughter, Annalise. She was named, in part, after my deceased mother. Jack thought it was a way to honor my mother; I saw it as a morbid reminder. Dead was dead. I didn't want to be reminded every day that my mother was gone. I didn't see the possibility that my mother could be an angelic protector of my precious little girl.

Annalise's name became even more of a sore issue when I was diagnosed with breast cancer. My mother died of breast cancer when I was fourteen, and I have been haunted ever since by my own predisposition. How many chips would I wager, if gambling were my game, on the odds of our genetics spitting out another female destined to be felled by cancer? My mother had only one daughter, which made me the sole target on the DNA dart board.

In a recurring dream, cancer comes disguised in a black hood, stalking the tinseled landscape between my wakefulness and sleep. What stroke of genius devised my destiny? What heavenly cynic trundled Annalise across the valley of unborn infants to be my child? Why? So she could be the next in line, another daughter in the familial legacy of lost breasts and early demise waiting for the past to repeat itself?

God knows I went to sleep trying not to think these negative thoughts, trying to hold fast to my last, thin thread of hope, but I awoke yesterday morning to find that all hope had vanished. The minute my eyes opened I could foresee nothing but my own death. I never wanted to end my life by my own hand, I never wanted to die young, but even without thoughts of suicide, it seemed that my demise was imminent, that I had no choices left. I must roll over for cancer. Let it win, let it take me.

If I had confessed this to Jack, he would have called me a drama queen, and he would have been right. It is true I tend towards the dramatic when there's a crisis. Some people gather their wits about them, sort through all the mire and come out on the other side transformed. This is an admirable quality, which I lack. Jack, on the other hand, is the one among us who sees only the silver lining. He is the motivator, the optimist, the Hud-we-can-get-through-this kind of guy a person like me needs.

I said this to myself still fully dressed, a continuous spray of water spilling off my scalp. It took a few minutes to unbutton my pajama top and pull off my bottoms. I worked the soap to create a rich lather and distributed it over my body. The fine smell of lavender filled my nostrils and calmed me. Water was good medicine. I felt its power forcing me to practice my limited knowledge of deep breathing and internal focus. Never quite clear on this concept, I struggled with exactly how to regain inner control, how to cope, if only long enough to fool Jack.

Two

Our kitchen is on the other side of the bathroom wall. I could hear the cranked up volume of the radio and the voices of my family working hard to be heard over the morning DJ and the Top Forty. The water was off and I stood dripping, watching the remains of the runoff being gulped by the drain. My pajamas glistened, a wet heap in the corner of the tub, and despite my concentrated effort to be in control, the compulsive side of me turned away, leaving the clothes to be dealt with by someone else.

An oversized towel hung on the rack next to the tub. I wrapped it around my shivering self, unable for the moment to take another step. My eyes rested on nothing in particular. The mere act of standing seemed to sap all my strength. This inertia could not persist, for Jack would come back. He would probably jimmy the lock this time to get in.

Hand over hand I moved the porous surface of the towel along each arm and my torso. The task seemed monumental. Seconds became minutes in my crippled effort to head off Jack's return. Successful, I reached for my bathrobe, half on and half off the small chair next to the tub. The towel fell to my ankles as I slipped into its terrycloth sleeves and balanced precariously, first on one foot, then the other to straddle the tub.

I'd come into the bathroom barefoot, and on a January morning this was not wise. My toes curled involuntarily, lifting a portion of each sole off the frigid floor. A quick series of hops got me to the door. When I opened it, there was Annalise seated on the bed cross-legged, combing the dog with her hairbrush.

My daughter has chestnut curls that bunch into thick clusters around her face and down her back. Yesterday the ringlets were profuse, a dense volume of auburn hues cascading to almost the length of her arms. Her singular beauty is of the quality that sweeps you up and shortens your breath.

"Good morning, Mummy," she said. "Daddy is cooking breakfast, but I'm not hungry. Will you do my hair?"

She asked her question and pushed her face into the dog's neck. He rolled over and his paws went limp, belly up, head and tongue slack and content. Annalise giggled into his fur. Her laughter was usually infectious. Jack and I often wondered how we spent so many years without knowing its melody. Our daughter's conception was unplanned—not unwanted, just a surprise. Three boys filled a house in such a way that the entry of a baby girl changed everything, and from the very second she joined us, we could not remember our life without her. In my heart, I longed for Annalise's coming, but I feared it with such intensity that I believed I had willed it not to happen, for without a daughter I could squash the passing on of breast cancer to another generation.

Something diverted my attention, a shadow in the periphery. I glanced up and caught a reflection in the mirror over the bureau: a watercolor blur of a black hooded form. Fear seized me. What I saw had to be an illusion. When the instant passed, and the demon disappeared, in its place stood a woman, wide eyes staring straight at me. I rubbed my bony orbs, seeking to erase my cancer-ravaged reflection. I could give in to my disease, but I wasn't going to be pleasant about it. The insult was too great. I was angry. Goddamn pissed.

Annalise watched openmouthed, her lips two perfect half moons.

She sat silent and straight.

"Aunt Kathy will fix your hair when she comes, honey," I said turning from the mirror.

"I don't want Aunt Kathy to do my hair. She pulls the elastic too hard and my hair hurts," she said. Her body language changed with a subtle softening of her shoulders, until each drooped against Yellow Dog.

Annalise and the dog looked at me with pleading expressions. The dark halo of Annalise's hair encircled the pair. The boys had picked our family pet from a neighbor's litter. Yellow Dog was the runt. Close to three years old when Annalise arrived, Yellow Dog immediately became her guardian. He followed her by day, and by night he stayed on the floor next to her cradle, later by her crib, and now he had become the security at the foot of her bed. We kept an oversized dog bed in the family room, but Yellow Dog slept there only when Annalise was out.

"Hair does not hurt, honey," I said flatly. "It's the skin on your scalp that gets pulled. That's what's uncomfortable."

Annalise's sweet face had a quizzical look. She pulled herself upright and moved off the bed, holding her brush in one clenched fist. Huge clumps of golden dog hair sprouted off its bristles. She walked over to me and dropped her hair elastics, adorned with bright plastic balls, into my pocket.

"Aunt Kathy isn't my mummy," my four-year-old daughter declared and ran out of my room with her unruly bed-hair bouncing in multiple directions, Yellow Dog at her heels.

Any day but yesterday I would have run after Annalise. I would have seen how ridiculous I was behaving, and I would have sat her on my lap and gently gathered her hair into a ponytail. Instead, the burden of her presence was lifted when she ran away. Rage bubbled like the chemicals inside me. I had reached my saturation point, my last straw, the end of my rope. Moving around the room, hunched of shoulder and slow of step, I talked to myself. I muttered expletives and railed at God for the injustice of having to die before my children were grown. There would be no future for me, no happy celebrations or occasions to share.

I continued to see my mirrored self as I dressed and blamed God for my misery. I turned my back to the reflection in defiance, attempting to hide my fear that the dark-hooded shape would reappear and wrest me away, robbing me of tomorrow, my daughter's fifth birthday, my last chance to see her blow out candles.

My shoes had traveled under the bed during the night. I sank to my knees, groping for one, then the other. Coming up from the floor, I paused and saw the sunken eyes and sharp angles of my thinned face traced atop a neck so narrow that it disappeared in the collar of my robe.

One shoe was on and one was in my right hand. I threw it into the mirror. A fierce sound cracked the silence around me. The shoe had found the exact center of my reflection. A fissure opened up, splitting my image in two, and the shoe appeared to hang, then made its final descent and inevitable crash to the bureau. Several bottles of perfume shattered, glass scattering in lethal fragments under, over and inside whatever was in the shoe's path.

The rain of glass was deafening. From all corners of the house, feet moved in haste, scurrying to find the source. Jack and the kids bounded into the bedroom.

I felt nothing. I wasn't sorry. I didn't see their anxious faces or hear their concern. I was done being preached to about being upbeat. Every jagged slice of the mirror was a splintered piece of me.

"Way to go, Mom," one of the twins said.

He could have uttered the forbidden *f*-word without reprimand. The aftershock of what I had done made everything else pale. I watched Jack's face crumble, his brows turning down into the furrows around his eyes. No words came out of Jack's mouth, twisted in disbelief.

"Bull's-eye," someone muttered.

"Boys ..." Jack was about to give an order. "Boys, go get the broom, dustpan, garbage can and vacuum cleaner. And put Yellow Dog downstairs." He said this with one breath. "Annalise, don't come any further. Go put on your shoes and finish your breakfast."

Jack then turned to me. He looked old, very old. All the good humor lines that had drawn themselves across his face were melded into one another.

"Hud," his voice was a hoarse whisper. "There is something going on here that I don't get. Something bitter and ugly has suddenly taken over my wife, my life."

"Cancer," I said.

"What?"

"Cancer, Jack. It's called fucking *cancer*. Tell me what part of that word you don't understand."

I looked over at the small valise that I took to the hospital with me on Tuesdays. "Don't worry, Jack, I'm not dangerous to myself or to the children, only to inanimate objects. The person looking back at me in that mirror was a stranger. I don't allow strangers into my house, let alone into my bedroom," I said.

"Our bedroom," Jack corrected me.

"Ours, yours, mine, what difference does it make?" I badgered him.

"Our bedroom," he said it again with more firmness in his tone. "It makes a difference to me."

Jack, dear sweet Jack, staunch in his support, despite my insensitivity.

The boys returned and the four of them began to clean up. I stood and watched for a minute. Not one of them spoke; their work needed no instructions. Jack acknowledged me hesitating in the doorway.

"Annalise needs you, Hud. Go to her."

He gave me the kind command and resumed the task of righting the chaos.

Kathy came through the back door as I finished pouring myself a cup of tea. "What's with all the long faces?" she asked.

"Do yourself a favor, Kath. Don't ask any questions today." I sipped my tea and blew across the rim without lifting my lips.

"Ouch!" she said. "Okay, well, the good news is my neighbor is going to pick up all the boys after school today. Early dismissal has been announced because of snow." Kathy took the sponge out of the sink and wiped down the counter. "Jack's taking Annalise to the marine lab and then to my mother's for lunch, and that leaves you and me free to go *shopping*." Kathy smiled at me and winked. She was implacable, full of hope, standing here in my kitchen day after day seeing to our needs, probably getting up an hour earlier to get her own family organized and then out the door to do the same for us.

I did not thank her. I searched instead my daughter's face for a reaction to Kathy's lie. What does my little girl know about chemotherapy? What does she need to know? Annalise moved her spoon in a zigzag design over her oatmeal. She wasn't listening to our conversation; she was singing to herself.

"Nice plan, Kath, but I'm going to Boston Women's alone," I said.

"Not today," she said and repeated, "not today."

The boys came into the kitchen. The broom and dustpan were put back into the closet and the twins hauled the vacuum cleaner downstairs into the playroom.

"So, you men are busy cleaning house today?" she asked.

"Something like that," Jack said as he walked past us, carrying neat bundles of broken mirror and several beloved knickknacks that had been reduced to splinters. He slowed his pace to kiss his sister on the cheek and continued into the back entry.

Kathy put two fingers on the imprint of his kiss and the corners of her mouth went up in that same half-grin that she shares with her brother, but just as quickly a frown formed and whisked it away. She leaned toward me.

"Hud," her voice was a whisper, "what's going on?" Kathy looked at me, her eyes brimming with questions, not one of which could or would be answered in front of Annalise.

"Aunt Kathy," Annalise interrupted.

"Yes, honey?" Kathy kept her eyes on me and tilted her head slightly to listen.

"You missed the boom," she said.

"Boom?" Kathy propped herself on her elbows, face to face with Annalise.

"Mummy broke the glass in her bedroom with her shoe."

All noise ceased. Jack had come back into the kitchen and shut the radio off. My sister-in-law stood upright, crossed her arms and peered at me. The boys had already gone outside and the echo of their laughter was muted, only the perk of coffee dared to be heard, its aroma already a presence.

"Boom!" Annalise said.

"I think I need to go out and come back in," Kathy said. "The full moon is making you all wicked crazy. It can do that you know, make you weird." She came over next to me, took my teacup out of my hand and moved toward the sink.

"Give it up, sis," Jack said, glancing in her direction then turning to his daughter. "Annalise, did the boom scare you, honey?"

My husband crouched down next to his daughter and took her hand in his. She didn't answer; more like her mother even at four.

"Do you want to tell Daddy about the boom?" he asked. Annalise shook her head. Jack sighed and sat back on his heels. He too shook his head, but his gesture was one of defeat.

Kathy reached across her brother and took Annalise's spoon with the swiftness of a magician, so quick that perhaps Annalise never knew it was out of her hand. She fed Annalise the last of her oatmeal, my child taking each mouthful like an infant in a high chair. After the last bite, Kathy took the dish to the sink, rinsed it out and put the bowl and the remaining dishes in the dishwasher. She then went into the bedroom to get my bag and must have stood for a few minutes surveying the wreckage. I knew her well enough to guess what went through her mind, the fears that she and Jack kept from me, the unspoken ones about my dying. All this was evident by the absence of color on her face when she came back.

"Kathy is taking me to Boston Women's, Jack." I said this to alter the mood, to prevent more damage.

He looked at me with tears in his eyes. Yesterday this did not break my heart. Today the thought of those tears cuts through me like a sword. He took my face in his hands and kissed me on the lips. His kiss was soft and full. I buried my face in his chest and kept silent. I kept all the words I could have said and should have said inside my head. Jack Emerald is a good man, a good father and a good husband. I should have told him that when I had the chance.

My mother often said, don't ever go to sleep angry or leave without saying I love you. I did not heed her advice, and now I'm in some kind of purgatory, shoved up against a damp pane of glass trying to make sense of the last twenty-four hours.

THREE

Kathy got my coat and held it out for me. She shouldered my valise, told Jack not to worry and steered me out the door. I didn't look back.

Her three boys had been waiting in the car, engine running, heat up, and the radio blaring. They must have gotten bored and got out of the van to play with their Emerald cousins. One of them had put a window down and music flowed out of the car onto passing currents of cold air. All the boys were now in the driveway, engaged in a pick-up game of basketball. Unperturbed by the relentlessly falling snow, one boy jostled while another pushed, dribbled and shot.

The kids were exhilarated by the anticipation of an early dismissal, and they climbed back into Kathy's van, making boyish promises to build a snow fort and a snowman for Annalise later on. My kids had forgotten the smashed mirror. As the young do so easily, my boys had let go.

We stopped at Gloucester High School, my former place of employment, to drop off Kathy's ninth grader. I should be my nephew's teacher this year, but I've been on a leave of absence since September. The Hudson Catalina who taught English Literature has had to put her old life on hold. Months have folded one on top of the other, and each has distanced me further from what I used to be, and made me what I am now. Not just my physical body has changed, but the *me* that had so many friends, the *me* that ran marathons, the *me* that fished off the pier with her sons, the *me* that lived life passionately, and the *me* that loved teaching.

Jack said taking the school year off would give me the time I needed to recover from surgery and chemotherapy. In the beginning I agreed with him, but as September became December, I began to think my leave was the time I needed to die.

The remaining kids were dropped off at the middle school and by then, pea-sized particles of ice and snow pinged against the windshield. In the parking lot, buses and cars clogged the entrance and exit. The weatherman's prediction was assured; Cape Ann should expect a heavy accumulation. Driving anywhere was risky. Driving to Boston was insane.

Kathy switched on her high beams and made a U-turn against traffic. Several cars braked in haste, blinded by surprise as she swung her seven-passenger vehicle into a southerly direction. We were both on edge from the morning fiasco, and she looked over at me, expecting my usual cryptic remark. "Don't say a word," she said out of the corner of her mouth.

I looked away from her pained expression and stared out the passenger window. My sister-in-law was my best friend. I didn't need to answer her. I didn't need to make her feel comfortable or search inside myself for traces of laughter that had not been poisoned by chemo.

"Thanks for keeping the wisecracks to yourself, and for letting me take you to the hospital today," Kathy said, touching my shoulder with a soft squeeze. Her hand trembled in the brief seconds that it rested there. She felt, I'm sure, the flesh move under her fingertips, and the sharp curvature of the bones devoid of muscle, but I was so detached from feeling anything that I did not acknowledge her discovery.

Settling into my seat I closed my eyes and ignored her attention. The ride to Boston Women's was about forty-five minutes without traffic. I had convinced Jack, Kathy, and my mother-in-law that I could do the drive on my own. It was my father, now living in Florida, who tried to pull the plug on my solo travels. He made a trip up to Cape Ann in October, and at one point took Jack aside telling him, in no uncertain terms, that I was not to go alone for my treatments. Victor Catalina had lived through a wife dying of breast cancer, and presumed his opinion mattered. My reaction to my father was that he should mind his own goddamn business. I would take myself, end of discussion.

My mother's dying and my fourteenth birthday occurred simultaneously. The events ran together, shortening my celebration and heightening my loss. Although my father had been stalwart in his support of my mother during her prolonged illness, I was angry that he would choose to displace my brother and me by sending us to live in Gloucester. It was inconceivable that Victor Catalina would put his children into the hands of his parents, in an apartment above their restaurant, in a place where we had no friends. He explained his concern for our wellbeing and for the toll that my mother's illness was taking on us as a family. I couldn't comprehend this and only learned years later that it was my mother who had urged him to send us to live with his parents.

My father and mother were soul mates, the often-sought-after-but-seldom-found kind. They met at Quincy High School when he was twenty and doing a semester of student teaching. Her name was Anna O'Malley, and she was barely fifteen years old. Victor Catalina kept his distance. How could he court a teenager? Letters became their means of communication, love letters that my mother kept for years, tied with a white silk ribbon. My father, an English literature major in college, had a gift for writing. He wrote sonnets of affection to Anna O'Malley, simple verses and long soliloquies all in the name of love. Their secret correspondence lasted three years, right up to the date of Anna's high school graduation. Two weeks later, without either having met the other's family, they eloped.

To look at my parents, you would never think that either of them could have been so bold, so outrageous. Victor with his owl-rimmed glasses and my mother with her prim bangs cut a whole inch above her eyebrows. They peer out of dated photographs with lips spread wide against their teeth. No trace of their passion is seen, no hint of the surge of rebellion that sent them across the state line in the middle of a June night to become man and wife. The mystery was part of their package, an intricate slice of the whole that was the two of them. Love is an amazing state of being; it can toss you high above reason without one thought of a safety net.

We lived in Fall River. Claire Laskey, my mother's dearest friend, lived near us with her one child, Peter. She had never married. Her son had been born *out of wedlock*, a term whispered behind fanned fingers and closed doors. Claire was a single mother long before single motherhood was vogue. No one ever asked about Peter's father, and no one ever volunteered information. I sometimes speculated but never dared speak my thoughts out loud. My mother's explanation was simple; what happened was best forgotten. Secrets have a way of vanishing, of becoming invisible. Anna O'Malley would not betray any skeleton in the closet, and went to her death with Claire's past sewn inside.

Claire was the reason my parents settled in Fall River. Victor and Anna decided that once married they would move to a place where no one would judge them. That Claire went on ahead looking for obscurity made the choice easier. Fall River was a blue-collar city with good people and job opportunities, two important criteria for calling it home.

After my mother died, my father turned to Claire for solace. No one else but she could come close to filling the hole in his heart.

If Victor knew Claire Laskey's history, he too would not divulge it. Two years after Anna O'Malley's death, my father asked Claire to marry him. When she said yes, it was because Anna O'Malley had made her promise to take care of all of us.

In the past twenty-four hours, I have had so much time to think, and that time has given many insights, one of which being the depth of my father's love for my mother. His affection had no beginning and no end. Like the old love letters carefully stored away, my father's love for my mother is, without doubt, still wrapped tight around his heart.

But all of these noteworthy characteristics failed to register in my brain when I was thirteen and my mother lay dying. All I knew or cared about was that my summer plans had been flung into confusion and turmoil. I was about to be uprooted from my school, neighborhood and friends, and sent to Gloucester, Massachusetts.

"Hud, what's going through your head?" Kathy broke the silence.

"I'm just thinking, Kath. Going back over a lot of things," I said. She drew in a breath, started to speak and changed her mind. Something in the way she reacted made me think of my brother. Martin, even as a man, still chooses to see only the good things in life, another optimist, like my sister-in-law.

My brother was nine years old when we moved to the North Shore. He gave my father no argument, no resistance. Marty loved the boats, the beach, fishing and the harbor on Cape Ann, but most of all he loved food. Living above Catalina's Bistro did not conjure up, for my brother, any of my preconceived ideas. I had envisioned living with our grandparents as a teenager, condemned to the old ways, old rules, old minds and worst of all, old odors. Smells that had nothing to do with appetite, like bread baking or sauce simmering, but the kinds of odors that only people over fifty have.

My brother thought the proximity to our grandparents' restaurant quite exotic. His stay, unlike mine, was uneventful, except for our mother's passing, and in its entirety lasted only two years.

When it was time to resume his former life and go back to Fall River with Victor and Claire, Martin went without a struggle. Wisdom was, and remains, his strong point.

We departed Fall River on the last day of school. Victor had loaded up his Mercury, a U-Haul hanging off its back end like an unstable caboose. He waited in the driveway for each of us to get off our respective buses. Marty and I barely had time to go to the bathroom and grab a snack before our father was honking the horn and shouting for us to get into the car.

I refused to sit up front next to my father, although there was enough room for the three of us without elbows touching. My brother, always the peacemaker, dumped his duffel bag onto the seat next to Victor and slid in next to me in the back. We stopped at the hospital to see our mother. The visit is etched upon my mind like a tattoo.

She was propped up on several pillows, a splash of color on her cheeks and lips. My mother smiled when she saw us; her eyes were bright, still holding on to hope. Her frail arms surrounded Martin and me as she told us how much fun it would be to stay on Cape Ann for the summer, how we must help at the restaurant, obey our grandparents and not worry about her. "Always remember I love you," she said. "No matter what, stay true to that. In the years ahead, I will be your guiding light. There will be no darkness in your life because I will always be up ahead showing you the way."

We returned to the car, my father making a huge effort to compensate for his pain and our vulnerability. He checked the tires two times, pulled at the hitch to judge its security, got in behind the wheel, turned on the ignition and sat quietly. No one spoke. Martin and I were slouched in the back and could not see his face; our view was the back of his head and the odd way his hairs cowlicked in two places off the crown.

Without warning, Victor shut off the engine, told us to wait and ran back into the hospital as if he'd forgotten something. Martin and I sat in silence for a few minutes, and then my brother said, "Hud, I think Mom is dying, don't you?"

Only my eyes moved before I responded. His youthful energy was uncorked next to me waiting for an answer: yes or no. I teetered onto a precarious place, the bridge between speaking the truth or telling a lie. I held my breath and waited so long to reply that my vision blurred.

On the day of my mother's surgery, my father had come home after so many hours of waiting. I had stayed home with Martin, and it was so late that Martin had gone to bed. Victor came through the front door, barely acknowledging me sitting in the living room. He walked as if someone had removed his internal compass, as if he'd never been inside our house before. I followed him into the kitchen and watched him get a glass out of the cupboard and dust off a whiskey bottle. He poured the glass about a quarter full, put it to his lips and threw his head back to catch the contents in his throat. After he swallowed, he grimaced and slammed the glass down on the table. He looked up at me, seeing me, I thought, for the first time. "I won't be able to live without her," he said and put his head in his hands and cried.

"Don't ask me junk I can't answer," I said to my brother

"Billy Sullivan's father died in his sleep, and Jimmy Costa's dog got run over by a car. Gone like that, Hud. Dead like that." Martin was kneeling on the back seat, his arms and hands churning.

"Do I look like the reincarnation of Jesus Christ, Marty?"

He shook his head, and I knew that all the cover-up, all the pretense and closed-door conversations could not keep the truth from spilling out eventually.

"All right, *no*, Mom's just real sick, and, well … it's going to take a lot of medicine and rest and doctors and us going away for her to get better." He listened, arms unwinding, taking in my words, processing them, calculating and weighing each syllable to be true or false.

Finally he said, "Okay, if you say so."

"I say so," I said, knowing it wasn't true, knowing that I'd lied to my little brother.

Our father returned and talk about our mother ended. By the time we crossed the bridge to Cape Ann, Victor and Martin were intent on listening to the Red Sox-Yankee game, zero-zero in the fifth inning.

Our grandparents, Joseph and Rose Catalina, lived a few streets off the wharf. Their home was a series of rooms above their restaurant. Each day the two of them would rise before the sun, descend the steps from their apartment above to their restaurant below, and get several pots of coffee brewing for their loyal breakfast customers. The day we arrived, our grandparents gave Martin my father's old bedroom and had cleaned out Grandma Rose's sewing room for me. A narrow iron bed frame was retrieved from their attic and a mattress delivered from Filenes in Boston. Their hospitality included three delicious meals a day, all of which I refused.

My mother's disease ruined my life, the only life I had known, and I hated her for it, and my father as well. I had decided to starve myself the minute my father packed the rented u-haul. This would make me so unhealthy that I would have to be hospitalized with my mother. My plan did not work. A teenager has two arms and two feet that can move a lot faster than those of her grandparents. Two weeks after our move, I was a staple at their seaport restaurant, washing dishes, sorting groceries and baking bread.

Joseph Catalina stood about five foot eight inches with a full head of gleaming, white hair. He had once been a fisherman and learned the pitfalls of ocean life early on. Grandpa Joe respected the men who made their living at sea, but he did not miss what he never cherished. Feeding them was his enjoyment. He often told me that my grandmother's fresh pasta, sauces and steaming meats were soul food, not the kind that made your feet tap or your hands clap, but the kind of food that kept your spirit alive.

I loved my grandfather. If it were not for him that summer on Cape Ann, I would have preceded my mother to the grave. Grandpa Joe saw through my brazen façade and knew how to coax smiles from my tight lips and belly laughs from my empty stomach. He would tie an apron around my jeans and dip my hands into a bowl of flour. His specialty was bread, and one of my chores was to measure out the ingredients: yeast, water and olive oil for his famous *ciabatta*. With nimble fingers, he would knead the dough, demonstrating his technique and being patient with my awkward attempts to learn. As we pounded and rolled the precious mix, he would tell me stories. I was never quite sure where the truth ended and his imagination began.

It occurred to me, on the drive to Boston, that my grandfather would not have allowed me to wallow in a dark place of refuge. Behind my closed eyelids, I shut down Kathy and the prospect of her well-intentioned babble. I rode instead with Grandpa Joe in his green Desoto.

"Did I ever tell you about my cousin Giovanni?" He asked.

My fourteen-year-old shoulders turned away from him in the front seat, and my eyes rolled back in my head, knowing that the question didn't require an answer. Grandpa Joe would just keep talking. It was as if my presence opened up a portal to his past. Short drive or long journey, he had a tale to tell about a relative with a family secret, or a friend in the First World War who dressed like a woman to escape the enemy. When we weren't driving, baking or working, he would sit me down on the over-stuffed sofa in the living room facing the ocean.

My grandparents' furniture had a history; every figurine, every lace doily and lamp came from someone or some place that infused it with memories. Grandpa Joe had a stack of photo albums that he kept on a low table in front of the old sofa. He would set his round body against the cushions' indents. One arm would rest on a worn patch of velvet under his elbow, and his other hand would pat the seat next to him, inviting me to sit and watch the sea. Sometimes Grandma Rose would come and join us, and at rare times my brother, who couldn't sit long enough to have a leg fall asleep.

His leather albums felt grainy to the touch with dark, worn pages marked by tattered edges that smelled faintly of *ribollita* and pressed flowers. I would run my palm across the faded photographs attached corner to corner with notched paper triangles. Relatives and siblings from the old country looked back at me with their stiff, powder-flash poses. Each face held a legacy of dark eyes, Roman noses, happiness and tragedy, their stories locked forever inside the history vault of my grandfather's mind.

"It is you, Hudson Catalina," Grandpa Joe would say. "It is you who will pass these stories on. You will tell my grandchildren and great-grandchildren about their roots and proud ancestors. You have a talent to teach, like your father. This is an extraordinary gift."

He believed in me that much.

FOUR

Strange how obsessed I was with death, and how my grandfather had ignored my penchant for morbidity by choosing me as the keeper of the family keys. If he were alive today, he would not accept that cancer was destined to kill me. Grandpa Joe made me the gatekeeper and, like the gods, I was supposed to be immortal. What I wouldn't have given to open my eyes and see him at the wheel.

Grandpa Joe pulled me from the brink of self-destruction, but he could not prevent me from spending the next twenty-four years in a periphery of fear, lying in wait for the beast—cancer—to strike. If he could have been at Ten Nettles Cove yesterday, I would have told him that I had become the woman in the mirror, the woman who let breast cancer win because she did not believe in herself anymore, that she and I were one, and together we had lost faith.

Kathy turned on the radio to listen to the weather. My reverie ended, exchanged now for news of school cancellations and travel advisories. The reality of a major snowstorm became more apparent as we made our way along Route 128.

"What were you thinking, Hud, when you threw that goddamn shoe at the mirror?" Kathy had been itching to ask me this question since Annalise tattled on me.

I opened my eyes, momentarily disappointed that we were not in a 1959 shark-finned mint-green Oldsmobile.

"I wasn't," I said.

"Wasn't thinking?" Kathy questioned. "You won't convince me, ever, that you *weren't*! Try again."

"Why?" My answer made her grunt. She banged the steering column.

"Jack says I need to be patient with you, but damn it, Hud, you're asking too much of him, the kids and me." Kathy's blinker click-clicked; she moved into the passing lane while continuing to chide me for my selfishness.

Under ordinary circumstances, I would have given Kathy the defense she sought. She and I were famous for our debates, often able to finish the other's thought or grasp a point without lengthy explanation. But having to explain my prevailing sense of doom to her seemed futile. I looked at Kathy Emerald's profile as she strained to see against the oncoming swirling gusts of snow. Fair-skinned like Jack, the years of sun and ocean were starting to show on the corners of her eyes and lips, but the wrinkles probably came more from laughing than squinting because she seldom frowned or found the serious side of life worthy of her time. This mind is small enough, she would tell me, too small to rent space to worrying.

What a blight to be surrounded by optimists.

My first summer on Cape Ann I met Mary Katherine Emerald as I rode my bike along the harbor. She was seated on a fisherman's tackle box painting her fingernails. I had stopped a few yards from her perch. My feet and legs were astride my bike and with my hands poised on the handlebars, I pretended to survey the boats in the harbor.

"Hey," she said.

"Huh?" I turned toward her. She had one hand out in front of her with fingers spread wide, in her other hand the polish brush. The painted nails got an air-drying shake and then a few gentle blows from her lips.

"What do you think of this color?" she asked me. My first instinct was to tell her to put her fingers where the sun didn't shine, but I thought about Grandpa Joe and how he kept telling me that in order to make friends I had to be a friend.

"Okay, I guess, if you're forty," I said. Her eyes went round, and her lips made an O and then went wide, up to her ears.

"You're a pisser," she said. She laughed and put the brush back into the bottle. She stretched her unpainted hand out to me and like a character out of a novel introduced herself. "My name is Kathy Emerald, little sister to the famous Gloucester High School basketball star, Jack "Bean Stalk" Emerald, daughter of Mary, a very large woman with a laugh that shakes the china, and sea-dog Francis "Frank" Emerald, a fisherman. Who are you?"

"The dying mother's daughter," I said. Kathy jumped up and ran to me. Her arms went around mine and then she squeezed me so tight I thought my ribs would crack.

"Don't mind me," she said, "I talk too much." She let go of me and stepped back to look into my eyes. "If you need a friend, we could give it a try."

Something happened in that moment. A metaphorical key turned and a rush of imprisoned words screamed out toward her for safety. I wanted to tell her everything, for her to know how my father had deserted us and gone back to Fall River alone. She was a good listener, still is.

She never believed that Victor had abandoned us. I was the only one who perceived him that way. Kathy Emerald let me rant and carry on without worrying if what she said would jeopardize our new friendship. She had a way of making me see both sides, to face up, and to recognize my complicity in each situation.

"Did you ever think how difficult all this is for your father?" she asked me one afternoon a few weeks after we had met. "Don't you think you should try to look at your mother's illness through his eyes?"

"Why should I?" That was how determined I was to be right. "Besides, I can't ask him because he's not here. He's never here."

"Just who do you think you are talking like that about your father, Hudson? Just who do you think you are?"

Twenty-four years have passed and she still asks me who I am. Just like yesterday morning, why did I throw my shoe? Isn't that the same as asking, *who do you think you are?*

Yesterday I didn't have an honest answer for who, or for what, I had become; skinny, cynical and breastless. But to my friend of so many years, I was still the twerp on a bike, and she was still Mary Katherine Emerald, despite her marriage fifteen years ago to her college sweetheart, Roy Fox. He was Boston College educated, born in New York. The fact that Kathy turned her city slicker into a beach boy is evidence of her uncanny ability to endear. Roy wouldn't go back to Queens for all the lobsters in the Rockport Fishery. There has been talk every so often of them going up to New Hampshire, but let that please be long after I'm gone.

"Okay, okay," I said. "No, I didn't think about what happens *after the shoe.* These days I don't think about consequences."

Kathy pulled her attention away from the road for a brief glance in my direction. Her dusty brown hair was stuffed into a woolen cap, and assorted stray strands fell over her cheeks and neck.

"Maybe you should start, this minute, before you screw things up so bad no band-aids or medicine will make it better," she said.

I didn't feel like arguing with my sister-in-law. The word *terminal* had lodged itself in my mind, and being terminal means you are the walking dead. Zombies are capable of making a plan, and mine was to take out the old pick-up when I got back home and head down to Whales Market. So what if Kathy was right about me mending my ways. At that moment, in her car, everything else seemed unimportant. She didn't know about my obsessed need to go to Whales Market. She had no knowledge of my plan to celebrate more than just Annalise's birthday at the party tomorrow—no one knew.

Aisle three in Whales Market was lined with every kind of bakery and party staple you can imagine. There were plates, cups, napkins, candles, balloons and dozens of other specialty items to turn an ordinary day into something special. That's why I needed to go there; that had been my plan.

"There are cupcakes in my freezer for Annalise's birthday tomorrow. I'm going to frost them later," I said. Annalise's cupcakes were more valuable than a request for forgiveness. Each of them needed a special decoration. My daughter was going to have milestones in her life that I would miss. She would take dance, play sports, graduate high school, go to college, get married and have children. All of these events required representation, acknowledgement and celebration before I died. To try to explain this to Kathy or to Jack would have met resistance. Each of them, in their own optimistic way, would have assured me that I was not going to die any time soon. That Annalise's fifth birthday was just one of many for me to celebrate. Neither Jack nor Kathy would understand. I could not convey to them, or to anyone, what it feels like to one day wake up without hope.

"Jack and the kids are going to my mother's. He told me to bring you there when we get back," Kathy answered, taking the turn marked Hospital.

"Please don't take me to your mother's. I want to go home. If I was driving myself, I would go straight home," I said, thinking that I could call Jack on the way back from chemotherapy and tell him to stay at his mother's house because all I wanted to do was sleep. The imagined conversation turned over in my head. Jack knew that the chemo made me gut-wrenchingly ill, and that I didn't want to be with anyone when I first came home from a treatment. The children knew this too, but trying to keep Annalise and Yellow Dog from curling up next to me was difficult.

"No, I won't take you home and let you stay there alone." Kathy pulled up the circular drive under the ornate portico of the main entrance. "Why do you have to give us such a hard time? Look what your family is doing for you, Hud. Besides, you just can't dismiss the whole shoe thing like it never happened. You *can not* do that."

"But the shoe thing is just pee-pee, Kath. What you and Jack won't face is that I'm dying. Who cares about a goddamn shoe?"

She'd come around to my side of the car, and was shaking the snow off her boots.

"What?" She looked at me, her face in a question mark. Tiny rivulets of melting snow rested on her long eyelashes. "I didn't hear what you said."

"Never mind," I said, not wanting to repeat myself or explain further. Unless she and Jack got inside my head, which wasn't an inviting place to be, neither of them would ever comprehend what happens when hope flees. My plan had to remain paramount. On the drive back to Gloucester, I would try one more time to convince her about taking me home.

"I have to meet with Dr. Hammer before they hook me up. Get some coffee and a newspaper and then come up to the third floor."

"That's gratitude for you, blow me off to the cafeteria while you rendezvous with Dr. Hammer, Hunk of the Year," she said, putting her hand on mine. Her body curved inside the car with an unspoken gesture of assistance. The parking valet came up beside us with a wheelchair as I stepped out of the car. He quickly recognized me and, without being asked, took the chair back inside.

"So, have you got everyone trained around here, or are they just afraid of you?" Kathy asked. She opened the back of the van to get my bag and her backpack and then handed off her keys to the same valet, joking with him as she followed me inside.

Kathy thought Dr. Hammer had walked off the set of an episode of ER, her medical version of a celebrity. My handsome oncologist's physical good looks were lost on me. He had been the surgeon responsible for removing my breasts: no points for him on my scoreboard. His reasoning was sound, despite current trends that rejected radical intervention. In my case, Dr. Hammer held strong to his belief that I would increase my chances several times over if I took an extreme approach to my treatment. The man was without question one of the best in the field of breast cancer. Jack backed his treatment plan one hundred percent and became my mouthpiece, my advocate and my savior.

The crooked finger of fate had stuck its tip into my mother's right nipple. Cancer took her life and was about to rob me of mine. The steep emotional climb I had been making since the age of fourteen was ending; the black-hooded demon and I had butted heads at last. The only part of me that could fight back was the Hudson Catalina that sat behind the steering wheel and drove herself to chemotherapy.

My father continued to chide me for being irrational and stubborn, two traits he repeatedly exhibited with recrimination and grim-lipped silence.

"You think you can do this alone?" Victor had said last October. "You are so damn thick-headed. Go ahead, be a smart ass. You've always been ready to beat me up. Telling anyone who would listen that I abandoned you and your brother. No one else in this family suffers from your resentment except me, your father, Victor Catalina. I'm going back to Florida. Jack can deal with you and your attitude, and you can do whatever the hell you want."

Not talking to me was his way of enforcing his opinion, but for me it was a relief.

"Good," I said to Jack, "I'm spared his incessant jabs at my meek attempts to regain some control over my fading life."

Jack grinned back at me with that sloppy smile that covered his face with abandon.

"Don't try to smile me out of this," I said. "Your wife is going to rent an airplane from Dusty Wallace with a written message unfurled off its tail saying Victor Catalina is a horse's petunia."

"A bit theatrical, Hud, don't you think? Let's tone down the Academy Award performance, please."

The whole drama queen thing again. The man saw right through me.

I retraced my usual Tuesday footsteps past the information desk, onto the elevator and up to the third floor. Kathy went down to the cafeteria and to the gift shop. Dr. Hammer's office was off a wide corridor at the front corner of the building. I went inside. There were floor-to-ceiling windows on two walls of his office that allowed both the doctor and his patient to have an unobstructed view of the ever-changing landscape. Over the past months, I'd watched leaves turn from summer green to autumn browns and orange. The once vibrant trees had fallen into a deep winter sleep, and yesterday I realized how close to death each of them had now come.

Dr. Hammer came into his office. His white starched lab coat was unbuttoned, and under it he wore a pale blue dress shirt and a silk tie imprinted with wallabies. Ordinarily I would have made some sarcastic remark about his choice of tie, some off-handed reference to the designer's possible identity. My doctor lectured all over the world; dozens of artifacts from his travels adorned his office, including this tie. Dr. Hammer was world-renowned, and I should have felt more secure in his ability as a surgeon and in his expertise, which had taken him to many continents. I should have genuflected, knowing that he addressed world health organizations regarding breast cancer and that he was asked to operate in Europe, Australia, the Far East and countries where women did not wear bras or even modest cover-ups. But I didn't feel more secure. Instead, I felt that he had robbed me, and all I could see, in spite of his worldly accolades, was tribal women, breasts sagging and nipples grazing their waists, lined up for mastectomies. He was not my hero.

"Good morning, Hudson," he said with a hand extended. "You defied the storm, brave girl."

I had been sitting with my legs crossed, watching the snow covering the wrought-iron furniture in the courtyard below. I shifted my gaze from his tie back to the window and left my hands on my lap. He withdrew his hand and sat on the corner of his desk, one foot dangling.

"I want to stop the chemotherapy," I said. "This will be my last treatment. I'm done with all the experiments and being a lab rat. I want to die in peace with hair and eyebrows."

Dr. Hammer's hands encircled his knee, and his Hollywood smile softened with compassion at my request.

"Have you spoken to Jack about terminating your treatment?" he asked.

The good doctor was placating me. He knew the answer to his question. Jack wasn't going to allow me to quit. My husband believed in the power of drugs, chemicals, radiation, infusion and central venous catheters. I got up and brushed past his foot.

"How many breasts did you cut off this morning?" I asked him. He walked over to me and put a hand on each of my shoulders.

"Chemotherapy is toxic, but not as poisonous as these negative thoughts you are having," Dr. Hammer said. "Hudson, you are a survivor. From the first day you and Jack came into my office, it was clear that you are a *fighter*. That quality of character can save your life." He had a piercing set of eyes that never strayed from mine. "As your doctor and your surgeon, I need to advise you against such a decision. Please, don't underestimate yourself, don't give up hope." I stepped back and his hands fell to his sides.

"It's too hard," I said. "I can't do this anymore. Hope is just a word. I've dropped it from my vocabulary."

My back was toward him now, and I had the door open. He stepped past me into the hallway as if to block my exit. He put one long arm out and rested his hand on the wall. "Hudson, please come back into my office so we can discuss this further."

I ducked under his arm and moved past Kathy who was sitting on the couch in the reception room. Our conversation ended, but I was curious how long it would take Dr. Hammer to try and reach Jack and tell on me. He pressed a button on the front desk to alert a nurse. Kathy got up when the good doctor did that, and the two of them exchanged a look.

Their escaped convict, that was what their look said about me, but in truth I was going only as far as the chemotherapy wing, not about to scale any electrified fences or fend off any guard dogs.

If Dr. Hammer wanted to tell Jack about yesterday's conversation, he would have needed to leave a message. Jack does not answer the telephone. My doctor had succeeded only once in getting my husband on the phone and that had been an accident, a coincidence, a twist of fate. My husband's office is on the third floor of our house. The space it occupies is filled with sunlight and has a wonderful cross breeze when the windows are open. He has shelves of marine specimens, a fax machine, a computer and one business line. Jack Emerald is quite proud of the specimens he's collected, is widely known for sending detailed faxes to his colleagues and respected around the world for his research, but his voice mail overflows and eventually fills to capacity. The people who know Jack well, know better than to call him.

Last August, Annalise and I had gone to the beach. The boys were at sleep-away basketball camp for two weeks, and we had been doing lots of mother-daughter things. We were just pulling into the garage when I heard the distant shrill of the telephone. I wasn't thinking about who it could be or why someone would call on a beautiful summer day at four thirty in the afternoon. I knew Jack wouldn't pick it up and I knew that I couldn't get into the house in time to answer before the machine picked up. The ringing ceased by the time I managed to get Annalise out of her car seat. Jack came to the inside door of the garage as I shifted Annalise from one hip to the other, her head limp against my shoulder.

"Hi, handsome," I said. "Will you take Annalise? She fell asleep in the car."

Jack looked like he had been sleeping too. He resembled a sleepwalker. His eyes were wide, and his hair was doing this straight-up-in-the-air kind of thing reserved for middle-of-the-night trips to the refrigerator.

"Have you seen a ghost, or did you answer the phone and get that *bad* news you are always worried about?" I chided him. He flinched.

"Take Annalise, please, Jack," I said again.

He moved towards us, took Annalise into his arms and walked back into the house. I finished cleaning out the car and hung the beach blankets and towels on the hooks installed for beach paraphernalia. Instead of following Jack inside, I took a fresh towel from an old cabinet on the far side of the garage. We have an outside shower and I needed to rinse off. There are lockers next to the cabinet with clean changes of clothes, underwear, socks etc. The beach is as much a part of our lives as the mountains are to some folk and city streets to others.

I stripped off my bathing suit in the small dressing area next to the outdoor shower stall and stepped inside. There was shampoo and crème rinse on a small shelf. I flipped open each one and turned on the water. The shower knobs are temperamental; you have to play with the hot water for about sixty seconds before you get it just right. Most times it doesn't matter whether the hot water is adjusted because a cool rinse is welcome after the sun and sand.

A fine mist of water covered me. I put the crown of my head into the spray and then raised my face so that its pelting wetness splashed over my eyes, nose and mouth. There is something about a shower that helps me to think more clearly. I crossed my arms in a self-protective hug, closed my eyes and let the water flow over my shoulders, hands, head and face. It rushed along my spine and found a way onto my buttocks, legs and feet. The water's voice drowned my own until I could put the pieces together.

I knew what was wrong with Jack.

There is an old saying that all of us have to face the stuff we fear the most, and my husband and I were headed in that direction. Everything in our world is ocean-related, so I think in metaphors of water. The tide comes in, sometimes clear and sometimes turned up by sea storms. That day I could feel a riptide, and it was going to take the legs out from under us. I had had two false-positive tests with mammograms over the past few years, brushes with the black-hooded demon as he, or she, sped past me on the way to someone else.

Two weeks before, I had gone in for my routine check-up. The technician assisting me was an older woman with soft white curls down to her shoulders. I thought she looked stunning with her dash of pink lipstick and no-dye hair. Her demeanor was kind and her hand gentle. I joked with her about how after every pregnancy my breasts seemed to get smaller. At some point, I said, they may not even fit your breast compressor. She smiled at me. There was a laminated tag on her flowered uniform jacket with the name *Grace* printed on it. The name fit her well; her eyes told me she was full of grace. Later, after the last of several additional views of my left breast, her eyes still held their shimmer of grace.

I turned the water off and stood drying in the late afternoon heat. Jack had answered the telephone while I was pulling into the garage. *I knew this was true.* He didn't tell me, but the words were written all over his face. My recent biopsy must have revealed malignancy. I closed my eyes and squeezed them tight and said a prayer to Anna O'Malley.

Jack was sitting at the kitchen table when I finally came inside. He had two glasses of iced tea in front of him and that patient look in his eyes that I fell in love with twenty years ago.

"You answered the phone?" I said to him. He put his fingers on his glass and its wet surface bled against each tip.

"Yes," was all he said, but there was so much more written into his expression.

We sat at the table without speaking. Jack was struggling with his composure. He bit his lower lip, his eyes fixed on the melting ice in his glass. Here is the wall, I thought, the one I knew I would hit someday. Maybe if I hadn't been so sure that I would die like my mother, maybe if I had not woven this destiny into my everyday life, maybe … maybe … maybe. But all the maybes were useless now. I had breast cancer. That was the bottom line.

"Dr. Hammer said we had to make a consultation appointment as soon as possible. He has the results from your biopsy. He didn't want to go into detail on the telephone, but he stressed that time was of the essence. I made an appointment for nine tomorrow morning."

He came to my side and put his arm around me.

There was no magic, no rabbits to pull out of a hat that would make the terrible news disappear. Both of my hands were on the table. I looked up at Jack and tried to smile. I turned each palm up to search for my lifelines. The highways of long and short, good and bad stared back at me. I focused on the arc across my thumb. It was longer than the others, stretching beyond their obvious ends.

Jack was away at college when he got the call that his father had been lost in a storm at sea. My husband's phobia about answering the telephone was born that day.

The Emerald family was one of many in this community who would lose a loved one to the deep. Widows' walks and the statue down at the harbor were created for this reason. It was a given that the life of a fisherman was dangerous, but no one dwelled on the possibility of a personal tragedy. Relying on the ocean for a living kept the families of fishermen anchored to uncertainty.

Jack Emerald took off a college semester to come home and help his mother. He was a fifth-year senior, majoring in marine biology, and after graduation he planned to join the research team at Woods Hole. Kathy and I had just entered college. I had been accepted at Salem Teachers' College as a commuter. Kathy was also a freshman but living on campus at Boston College when the news of Frank Emerald's passing came.

As a teenager, I had a crush on Jack, he was my best friend's cute brother, and I saw him almost every day. My outward affection for *Bean Stalk* Emerald was that of a sibling. Jack treated me like family, and I was sure, in the big picture, that this eliminated me from the prospect of becoming his wife. Kathy and I would go to his basketball games and cheer for him, dribbling the ball across the court, agile and fluid, sinking every shot. He was on a Massachusetts State team, which kept the soon-to-be first-year-scholarship athletes in shape. Kathy would wear his letter sweater, flaunting her little sister superiority over the females who were *Bean Stalk's* fans, and both of us would sit right behind the bench during the games.

Jack never had one special girlfriend. The plan was to save his heart for the right girl. His sister and I thought that this was pure drivel, but we humored Jack by agreeing with him. He left for his full ride on the West Coast when Kathy and I were freshmen in high school. His visits home over the next four years were brief holiday events. We heard rumors about a love affair or two, but he never brought anyone home to meet the family. He stayed in California each summer, working and traveling the Pacific.

Life has so many unknowns, as when love finds you when you are not looking for it, and I am certain that Jack and I would not have explored a relationship beyond big brother friendship had it not been for Francis "Frank" Emerald's death. Jack's father loved the ocean more than his wife. He loved it more than his children and more than the house on Marsh Road. In this, Mary Emerald took comfort, knowing that her husband was a seafaring man and that it was fitting for his grave to be at the bottom of the ocean. The family chose to have a memorial Mass for Frank at Our Lady of Good Voyage Church. It was packed with mourners from the neighborhood, the harbor and town hall, so many that Prospect Street was closed during the service. My father came from Fall River with Martin and Claire, and my grandparents closed their restaurant, choosing to feed instead Kathy's family, friends and acquaintances. The Catalina clan mixed with the Emeralds; we shared food and stories that honored the rites and rituals of a watery passage. Mary Emerald cried all day, her tears mixed with sobs and her tears mixed with laughter. She had a box of tissues under her arm the whole time, and some kind soul emerged at intervals to replace it when emptied.

In the few weeks that Kathy had been at college, I could see changes—her hair was shorter, her freckles were covered with foundation and her eyelashes layered thick by mascara. I watched her the day of her father's funeral, make-up intact, dry-eyed, moving among the guests with her engaging chatter and ready handshake. In all our years of friendship, she had cried only once, and that was the day that Jack flew out of Logan Airport to Los Angeles. She had rested her forehead on the window looking out onto the runway, and as the plane pulled out of the gate, she let go a flood. Jack waved from a window seat, and I waved back, blowing kisses, but Kathy was gone, her wrenching emotions washing down the glass that separated her from his departure.

When her father died, there were no tears, no moment of breakdown. Kathy stayed for two days and then returned to school with a breezy goodbye. She told me later that the four years she lived alone with her mother and father, when he was not captaining a boat, was enough familial bonding to last her a lifetime. Once she had taken up residence away at school, she was done. It was not that she didn't love them, but that the two of them had drained her emotionally.

A few days after Kathy returned to school, Jack came by the restaurant with a basket of Mary Emerald's preserves and soda bread. There was no way he and his family could ever thank Joe and Rose for their kindness, he said, the basket was just a little something.

I was at the kitchen table upstairs studying as Jack came up the back steps from the restaurant to the house. Grandpa Joe had sent him up there to put the basket on the counter. We made tea, and the two of us sat and talked until we heard footsteps on the stair treads. The door to the porch was open, and a salty breeze fluttered the curtains as Jack rose to greet my grandparents. He thanked them again for their generosity and then turned to ask me if I would take a ride with him over to Crane's Beach. He was heading up a volunteer study program for the preservation of the dunes, and perhaps I might like to go along.

My stomach did one of those funny flip-flops, a warning sign that something was about to happen to my heart. I slipped my sweater off the back of the chair and closed my book on early childhood development. Grandma Rose smiled at the two of us and in a few quick movements filled a lunch bag with snacks—a half-stick of dried sausage, a small loaf of *ciabatta*, four hard boiled eggs, a jar of black olives, two slices of Mrs. Wulinsky's peach pie and a thermos of lemonade. Maybe Jack Emerald fell in love with Grandma Rose that day? Or maybe she knew before either of us that love was coming.

That was the first of many tag-along work trips I did with Jack that fall. We used the time to get to know each other independent of our past. Jack was full of ambitious plans for his career in oceanographic research, and I was more of an ear, the familiar-faced listener, for all of his marine reform ideas.

On my birthday that October, Jack took me out to dinner in Boston. Up until that night, our dates had been casual, and the closest we had gotten to intimacy was holding hands. Jack arrived a few minutes early to pick me up and was sitting on the couch with Grandpa Joe, looking through a photo album, when I came into the living room ready to go. Jack's head was turned away from the doorway as I entered. Grandpa Joe saw me first. He whistled, and Jack turned in my direction. My hair was loose and fell over my shoulders to the middle of my back. The black silk dress I wore was new. Maybe it was my imagination, but I swear that Jack Emerald started to cry. His right hand went up across his cheek and then to his nose. He stood up, and Grandpa Joe did the same. Both men told me I looked beautiful.

Jack chose a place that overlooked Boston Harbor with a perfect table for two. We lingered over dinner for hours, our bodies leaning deeper into the middle of the small table, shoulders curved, fingers touching. A piano played in the distance, a series of soft romantic melodies that etched themselves into our memories. Our first kiss was outside the restaurant on the narrow deck that jutted out into the water. Jack took a small gift-wrapped box out of his jacket pocket and handed it to me. Inside was a single pearl on a thin gold chain. He told me how he had found the pearl on one of his ocean ventures. He had saved it, not knowing for what or for whom, but he said he would know when the time came. Jack asked me if I remembered how Kathy and I had made fun of him for saying he would save his heart for the right girl. I said yes, I remembered, and Jack said the right girl was Hudson Catalina.

Reciting this makes me wise, but a day late. I walked away from Dr. Hammer yesterday with the same indifference I had felt throwing the shoe in the mirror.

It took five months for me to dismiss hope, to slam the door and pull the covers up over my head. Jack has never, not for one minute, given up. He has become an even better listener than before. He writes down every question, clips articles and surfs the internet daily. The day we had our first consultation with Dr. Hammer, Jack was prepared to do whatever it would take to battle breast cancer. Immediately after the appointment, our first stop was the local health food store where Jack bought two cookbooks and changed our diets. He purchased special foods to increase my stamina and instituted a health regimen using vitamins and other alternative options. Hudson Catalina Emerald was not going to lose the battle. Jack's wife—me—was going to survive.

SIX

Jack and I had managed the diagnosis well in the beginning. Every appointment, every test, each surgery and the first several weeks of chemotherapy went fine, until my implants failed and the experimental medication began. Every day that followed, I hit one obstacle after another. Dr. Hammer and Jack ignored my pleas to stop the treatments. They had concurred on my course of therapy and the vote was two to one. I was to continue with the trial program that focused on more aggressive types of breast cancer. Saving my life could also save someone else's, but that kind of rhetoric had become old to me. Yesterday I resigned myself to complete one more session and after that, no more. Jack and Dr. Hammer had met their adversary and it wasn't cancer. It was me.

The chemotherapy area is on the same floor as Dr. Hammer's office. Windows across one wall look out onto the Boston skyline. Long rows of upholstered lounge chairs are lined up to face the view, front-row seats, reserved for patients. Women in various stages of "recovery" sit tethered to tubing that flows from cure-filled plastic pouches. Many of the faces are familiar.

Carol Goldstein is fifty-three years old, her second time in ten years battling the beast. She holds a chair for me next to her, like a kindergarten best friend. She talks, and I listen. Carol has a very mystical outlook on life, a mix of her orthodox roots and open-minded spirituality. I tell her I stopped believing in God, and she pats my hand and tells me to look inside myself. She tells me that is where God resides. If I can believe in that, I can believe in me.

I scan the room for other faces, instinct prompting me to check for the missing and ask about the dead, my morbid pastime while I am a part of this vignette. Some of the patients amaze me. I envy the ones who treat their chemical infusions like a stop for gas. These are the people who still go to work, wear carefully combed wigs and never get nauseous or constipated. Not me. I am your Murphy's Law example of multiple side effects. I suffer with neuropathy, mostly in my arms and fingers, which makes me a regular sideshow for the kids.

My pain medication has to be taken by the clock. If I miss, as I did yesterday, the pain is excruciating. Depression and confusion have partnered in my body; each has its hold on me. I know that despite taking Dr. Hammer's prescribed mood drug, I am still in a spiral, and that the depression related to my disease has compromised my attitude and is probably the reason I imploded yesterday. Intellectually I can understand everything that is happening to me and around me, but emotion makes me incapable of using logic.

"How are you doing today, Mrs. Emerald?" a sweet-voiced receptionist said, sliding the glass enclosure open to greet me. I guessed she had been the one Dr. Hammer buzzed, and perhaps she had sent the red alert out and was just waiting to see what I would do next.

I smiled at her through clenched teeth. Kathy came up beside me and I turned towards hers, the fake smile still on my lips.

"What the hell happened back there?" she said. "I can't believe you, Hud, the shoe and now Dr. Hammer. You have got to put the brakes on, step back and look at what you're doing." She was juggling a coat, hat, coffee, two newspapers, backpack and a cell phone.

"I'm here, okay? Leave it alone for now, Kath," I said. "Where's your sense of humor, anyway?" I laughed for the first time since I got out of bed.

"You're impossible," she said, reaching into her bag and pulling out a deck of cards. She grinned. "I thought we could play a little Canasta."

"We don't play Canasta," I said, feeling a fragment of my old self enjoying her joke. Her face looked surprised, like I'd just given her classified information. "No cards, today," I said, "I want you to get over the Dr. Hammer thing and meet my friend Carol. I've told her about you."

A nurse came for me before Kathy could answer, my escort in case I tried to slip away. We went ahead into a side room where I could undress from the waist up. I slipped on my hospital gown and went back out to Kathy. She had gone before me into the treatment room and made her own introduction to Carol Goldstein. The two of them were deep in conversation when I plopped down in my saved seat.

"Good morning, Hudson," Carol said reaching for my hand. "I am so delighted to at last meet Mary Katherine."

No one called Kathy by her full name except her mother, but I expected nothing less from Carol Goldstein. She had a way of speaking and looking straight into your eyes that left you feeling naked. I could tell by the expressions on each of their faces that Kathy had already given Carol the inside version of the shoe-in-the-mirror story and my escape from Dr. Hammer. The morning's headlines, besides the snowstorm.

My fake smile came out again as two nurses set up my treatment. I hated getting started. My body seemed to lurch, my stomach tensed up, and I could see myself hanging out of the car in a few hours, throwing up. Even with medication, the queasiness still won out. It was my secret and another reason to travel alone. I began calling the brake-down lane along Route 128 Vomit Highway. If I told Jack, he would insist on coming with me on Tuesdays, or send Kathy, or, worse yet, his mother.

"Hudson, dear," Carol Goldstein was speaking to me, "Mary Katherine tells me you are not having a very good day." Her hand still rested on mine, warm and smooth. "Don't be cross at her for telling me," Carol said in her soothing tone. "The more you flail, the tighter cancer's grip."

Kathy had seated herself on the floor between us. She had arranged all her belongings in a semicircle and was now cross-legged with snow boots as props for her elbows. Carol Goldstein was speaking and Kathy was a rapt listener. I closed my eyes when she got to the part about cancer's grip. My whole defense yesterday was no defense. Carol and Kathy went on talking to each other and let me alone.

This disease has made me compulsive, and I obsess over the least bit of minutiae. I was trying to think of ways to stave off my post-chemo illness long enough to do my round trip to Whales Market. The store is open seven days a week, in rainstorm or blizzard. Ruby Desmond, Whales' sole owner and manager, lives above the market and does not close, even on Christmas.

I calculated what needed to be done for my cupcake mission to work: a few hours here at the hospital, another one hour possibly back to Cape Ann, my convincing take-me-home speech with Kathy, my talk with Jack at his mother's, the drive into the storm to get what I needed at Whales, and then back to Ten Nettles Cove before my next dose of medication. I went over each scene a dozen different ways, right down to my conversations with Kathy, Jack and Ruby Desmond. If there was going to be a glitch, I must be prepared for it.

No amount of strategy would have prepared me for what was yet to come. At thirty-eight years old, I should have been more perceptive, should have known that life takes you off course. I had wanted to celebrate Annalise's birthday not for my daughter but for me. My plan to display one special life occasion on each of a host of cupcakes would have been unfair to Jack and to the children. Unfair because they still had hope. It is just as well it never happened.

Carol Goldstein had not taken her hand off mine. She gave it a squeeze, and I opened my eyes. Kathy was speaking to her in a subdued tone, crying for the second time in almost a quarter century. Carol leaned back in her chair, her head tipped to one side, as if she were thinking of the reply to a difficult question. Perpendicular creases were drawn along her cheeks. The color had drained from her skin, and her dark eyes were watery and sad. Neither of them noticed me watching them, one engrossed in talking, the other in listening.

I observed Kathy and Carol, witnessed their faces unmasked, saw how deeply cancer had penetrated their beings. Kathy was speaking about Jack. She told Carol Goldstein how afraid he was of losing me, how Jack cried in his car, his office, the shower—anywhere—when he was alone. Her freckled complexion was blotched red by her emotional confession, her voice raspy with sobs. "My brother tries to stay calm," she told Carol, "he refuses to take personally any of the crap that Hud dishes out. This disease has us all by the throat," she continued, "and Jack's always the first and the hardest hit."

Kathy once visited my mother in the hospital. She came with me to witness how cancer was killing not just my mother but the whole family. It was the second of my three visits that summer. Grandpa Joe drove us to Fall River, a trio in the Desoto's front seat, as wide as it was long, without seatbelts, eating Grandma Rose's prosciutto with provola sandwiches.

My mother had never met Kathy Emerald. I didn't know what to expect when we arrived, how my mother would look or act. I had become so dissociated from her as a whole, so disconnected, that

I wasn't sure when we got there if it was a good idea. Kathy was more serious than I ever remember her to be, and for most of the ride she was quiet. Mary Emerald had sewn my mother a bed jacket made of yellow chenille. It had a plastic angel button at its neck, quite amazing for Anna O'Malley, decades before angels were a fad, before they were worn on lapels and collars as protection. Thinking about it now I can see so much, but on that August day, I was, for the most part, blind.

Chemo for metastatic breast cancer was adopted in the nineteen seventies. How fortunate for Anna O'Malley. Her life was probably prolonged for nine or ten months because of it. Radical mastectomies were the rage, and since mammograms were a relatively new way of detecting breast cancer, abnormalities were often not detected the way they are today. Doctors surgically removed breasts, tumors, lymph nodes—everything. The woman we visited that summer, my mother, had endured all of these treatments, and still she clung to life.

Anna was resting when we arrived. Days and nights of painkillers and nothing to do but think and sleep, she lay motionless under her hospital coverings. The only part of her body visible was her small head with soft ringlets of returning hair lacquered to her scalp by perspiration. Awkwardly we stood at the foot of her bed, prepared perhaps to wait for an undetermined amount of time. A nurse came in and made a big deal of her visitors, enough so that my mother was forced back from the pain-reduced place that infused narcotics take you.

The nurse asked us to step out of the room while she ministered to my mother. Grandpa Joe found a chair to sit on; he didn't look well. I asked if he was okay, and he just nodded. Kathy and I split a piece of gum and watched the nurses go back and forth. What struck me most was the odor, the stench of illness and decaying bodies. I stretched my t-shirt up to my nose, as if to pull it over my head. In a short time the nurse motioned for us to return.

Anna O'Malley had undergone a transformation for her visitors. Grandpa Joe wrapped his strong arms around her and opened the basket from Grandma Rose. He spread a red checkered tablecloth from the bistro over her blanket and laid out, buffet style, all the delicious treats he and my grandmother had made. Carefully he broke off a piece of crust from our most recent batch of *ciabatta*, giving it to my mother to nibble and telling her how adept I'd become at kneading and measuring. She sampled each selection despite the visible sores on her lips and those unseen inside her mouth.

Kathy stepped forward and introduced herself. She saved me again. Grandpa Joe and Kathy helped Anna put on her bed jacket. The color illuminated her face and its nubby surface made her appear ten pounds heavier. My mother brightened with the addition of her canary robe. The mood became jovial and our insecurity faded. Anna O'Malley and Kathy Emerald liked each other in such a way that some might think they had known each other before, perhaps in a past life where I did not exist. It tugged on me, widening the already huge gap between mother and daughter.

I think today that my mother and I could not articulate our feelings. The pain was so close to the surface that we dug trenches around it, moats to keep us from having to feel the searing truth. We skirted the reality that my mother was going to die, that she would never see me as a grown woman. The truth was that Anna O'Malley would not see me graduate from high school, college or get married. Not one of my babies would call her grandma or cuddle in her arms. My mother knew all these things, but saying them out loud was impossible.

Our visit became festive. Laughter punctuated the room and stole down the halls into other hospital rooms. Heads peeked in every so often to listen, or be asked to join us. My mother had become the darling of the cancer ward, another fact lost on me. The people stopping by that day were her in-house friends. Anna O'Malley had begun a network among the patients, a connection that brought hope to each person she touched. The knot my mother formed was a forerunner of the kind of support groups that became available years later, the kind that sought my membership, long after my mother's demise. She and my father were favorites of the doctors and medical staff. Victor was often called upon to sit with a family member and talk them through a bad day, explain how a husband can help his wife through the aftermath of a mastectomy.

A tall, dark-haired girl in whites was among the revolving-door visitors in my mother's room. She seemed too young to be wearing a nurse's uniform, and whether it was for that reason or some other, she found her way over to me and started talking. From the outset, it was clear she was one of Anna O'Malley's biggest fans. After introductions were made, there was no shutting her up. I have a penchant for getting people to talk, they gravitate to me like fruit flies to a bowl of cherries. In the beginning, I half listened to the girl's banter. When she mentioned my father's role as an unofficial family *counselor*, I switched my attention one hundred percent. Here she had hit a raw place, the open wound that could not heal.

Victor Catalina—my father, the man who I was positive had abandoned his own children—was now the husband-father hero of the Fall River Hospital cancer ward! These insights into my parents should have given me some relief, but I wasn't interested in how brave they were as a couple or how kind each was to others in similar circumstances. I only cared about myself. I saw my father's time spent with strangers' children as one more reason to hold onto the boulder-sized chip I carried on my shoulder.

I couldn't bring myself to sit on my mother's bed, not right away, not while all those people came in and out of her room. But as the afternoon waned, I did eventually sit down, and from my corner of her bed I had a perfect view of Anna's face. I saw without obstruction the way her eyes gleamed. She would steal a quick look at me now and then, as if she didn't want me to know she was looking at me. Once I held her eyes for a few seconds; her expression told me so much in that moment, so many things I have only just begun to comprehend today. My mother loved me. She mouthed the words as our eyes met. But it was a different time, a different generation. Decisions had been made that I couldn't understand. *Remember me,* her eyes said. *We are not as distanced as you think. I am with you all the time.*

We were back in the car, the three of us lined up in the Oldsmobile's front seat. It was clear from their body language that Grandpa Joe and Kathy did not share my negative view of our visit. If I had wanted them to come away more convinced than me that the Catalina children were abandoned, I was wrong.

"Can you believe all those people going in and out of Anna's room?" I asked. "She cares more about them than about Marty and me. And all that stuff about Victor helping other families, what a bunch of junk that is. Who has seen good old Victor since he dropped us off two months ago? I guess your own kids don't count," I said.

Grandpa Joe didn't say anything. His face was pinched and his lips tight. Kathy was sitting next to me and shoved her elbow in my side.

"You need to lighten up on Victor," she said. "Give him some breathing room. Your father is a saint, for God's sake." She drummed this point into my head while getting enthusiastic nods of agreement from Grandpa Joe. His approval rating of Kathy Emerald soared that day.

"I can't even imagine what Frank Emerald would do in a similar situation," she said. "He'd likely book a passage on the slowest boat out of the harbor for starters."

After she lectured me about my father she never said another word. Kathy stared out the window. She and Grandpa Joe gave me the silent treatment. They gave me time to mull over what was said. But it has taken me more than twenty years to achieve clarity of thought.

I turned my attention back to Kathy and Carol. The confession about Jack's emotional meltdowns was for certain precipitated by the morning's events. Neither Kathy nor Carol was aware that I had heard any of their conversation. The telling of family secrets is not something Kathy would do lightly. She just wanted some answers. I knew that. Kathy wanted answers she couldn't get from me or her brother. So I watched and listened to her do the only thing she could, and that was to wait patiently for Carol Goldstein to offer her some piece of solace or wisdom. Carol opened her eyes, then closed them, perhaps looking into their veined membranes for answers. When she finally focused on Kathy, Carol's voice was stronger and a returned color sat high on her cheeks. She suggested that Jack continue to get professional counseling, that Kathy should remind him the disease was not about him or out to get him, and it wasn't questioning whether he was a good man. Cancer instead was asking him to be mindful of what his wife needed.

Kathy swallowed hard and blew her nose. It was then that both of them looked at me—one synchronized movement of two heads turning in my direction.

The spell was broken. Two sets of eyes cut through me like scalpels.

"How long have you been listening?" Carol asked me.

"Only a few minutes," I used the half-truth to lessen my embarrassment. Kathy had put her hand to her mouth when she realized I'd heard her confession about Jack.

"It's okay, Kath, I'm sorry. Just write today off as a shitty one for Hudson Catalina," I said. She smiled. What strength it took to do that.

SEVEN

I realized much later, well into last night, that Kathy's confession was meant for my ears. Everything that happens has a purpose, an underlying meaning or message that, if we listen, we can take like a puzzle piece and fit it into our life. Not aware of that yet, I shifted my stare away from them to the window.

The Boston skyline had disappeared. A white canvas replaced the view, waiting for the next artist or architect to revise its outline.

Kathy and Carol turned their heads to follow my gaze. Kathy took in an audible breath and let it out with an "oh my God."

Nothing moved outside. Nothing but the swirling snow. We were a rapt audience for the feature-length snowstorm being projected in front of us. I turned back to Carol.

"I can't believe what I'm seeing. We all have to get home. How did you and Irwin get here today?" I asked her.

"Irwin and I took a cab. He's waiting downstairs for me." She seemed less surprised by the disappearance of the skyline than Kathy or me. "Irwin will see to it that we get home safe. I'm not worried."

Irwin was Carol's husband, devoted and constant. He never came up to the treatment area, but stayed in a waiting room as if she was just shopping or getting her hair done. He read his papers and nodded to people going in and out. She told me that during the long course of her therapy, Irwin befriended the security guards, shopkeepers and nurses going on and off their shifts. He told stories, the same stories over and over to each new ear, always emphasizing his fondness for his wife, his bride, and the love of his life.

She had not aged in his eyes. His wife remained the perennial eighteen-year-old college freshman, the same young woman he had first met as she crossed the Brandeis campus on her way to art history class. Carol and Irwin were students of enduring love. They never took their love for granted. Their marriage was a work in progress. We are two people, she once told me, bound by promises made under a Hoopa many years ago.

"Hudson ..." Carol was still speaking.

"Yes," I said, knowing that Carol Goldstein wasn't ready to let me off the hook for what happened with my family earlier in the day.

"I need to tell you," she put her hand up to my face. "Hudson, this is not like other Tuesdays, you have nothing to prove today. Every week you come here alone, determined to prove to yourself, not to anyone else, that you don't need a hand to hold."

"You think I'm pretty pathetic, don't you?" I said. "What would you say if I told you that I'm not out to prove anything, that I just want it to be *my* life and not the life that someone else says is my life."

"I'd say thank goodness you have Mary Katherine to drive in this weather." She smiled at me then, smiled in that way that said she knew me, sort of like Grandpa Joe knew me. Carol could see through my thin skin and my bravado, but would never let on.

Kathy and Carol traded phone numbers and we all went down to the lobby together. Irwin had their cab waiting. Carol hugged the two of us and we watched as she and her husband got into the taxi and moved out from under the portico into the storm.

Our ride back to Gloucester took two hours. We were silent through most of the drive. All the words waiting to be spoken were left unsaid. The storm slowed traffic down to one lane, and high winds blew snowdrifts across the highway. Cars that had skidded and spun out were on the sides of the road, looking like double-jointed acrobats in a surreal circus. Kathy had to stop four times so I could open my door and lean my head out into the swirling, white gusts. My chemical cocktail had made its route through my system and, as if on cue, it surged upward, volcanic and boiling. Any thought of food intake was far from my mind, but Kathy had not eaten since breakfast, and when she's hungry, her disposition gets testy.

"I need food, Hud, there are sandwiches in a cooler under your seat," she said. I handed her a peanut butter and marshmallow, our favorite among the choices of what to put between two slices of white bread. Grandma Rose would never understand. She thought marshmallow was for hot cocoa and ice cream sundaes.

Kathy rallied. Her prime concern was for our safety and she pretty much ignored my persistent need to retch. The weather had proven to be far more paralyzing than either of us had imagined. She wanted to get back to her family and get me into a warm house. Any fears I had that Kathy Emerald would take me down the narrow roads leading to her mother's disappeared. I knew that my plan to go to Whales Market could happen, would happen.

My hat dripped onto my already wet parka. Snow had gotten inside the car each time I was sick. Small, tide pool–like puddles formed on the floor mats and door handles. I peeled off my gloves, soaked with the contents of my stomach, and tossed them out the window. The wind took them upward, spreading each finger wide before taking them away. Kathy chuckled without taking her eyes off the road ahead.

"Tuck your hands inside your sleeves," she said, like a mother to a child.

I explored her face with half-closed eyelids, unable to make small talk, unable to say a simple thank you. My hands were cold. I looked down at them, not sure if they were mine. The fingers were narrower than I remembered. There was a deathly dark aura above my knuckles and along my wrists.

My hands, I thought, were my mother's hands, the ones I remembered during my third and final visit to see her in the Fall River Hospital, this time in a room without windows. Everything about the space around my mother looked temporary, as if at any moment stagehands would come out from the wings and change the set. Her arms rested on the sheets, black and blue against hospital white.

I recalled resisting the impulse to draw close to her bed, as on previous visits, not wanting to be there, unable to look at her, so I focused on her hands. They were no longer covered with recognizable flesh; instead, long arcs of purple shadows ran up and down her fingers and all the way to her elbows. She called to me, her voice nearly indistinct.

"Hudson." She took in a shallow breath. "Hudson, come sit here." She tapped the sheet with one finger, but I remained frozen, my eyes locked on her hands.

The voice and those hands, I thought, could not belong to my mother. My father, standing behind me, put a fist on my back, and pushed me to a chair next to her bed.

"This is so unfair to you, Hudson," my mother said. "I am so sorry that this sadness is in your life."

I looked at her when she said the word sadness. Tears streamed down her delicate face. That was the last time I saw my mother breathing, the last time I heard her speak my name, and the last time I had the chance to hug her, which I didn't. Victor's fist pushed against my back again, but no one could make me cry or make me collapse on top of my mother's bird-like chest the way, deep inside, I wanted to with all my might. Instead, I sat there sullen and blank-eyed, and felt the sadness rising in me like a river set to overflow its banks.

"For God's sake, Hud, can't you hear me?" Kathy said, tossing her cell phone into my lap and jarring me out of my thoughts. "Call Jack. This storm has me scared to death."

I picked up the phone and dialed my mother-in-law's house, knowing that even on a good day it was a gamble trying to get a signal. The *No Service* feature came on assuring me I was correct. I looked at Kathy. Her shoulders were pulled up tight and her hands clenched the steering wheel.

"The phone isn't working," I said, "but I'll leave it on in case an incoming call manages to get through."

We could pray, I thought. That's what people do when faced with impossible odds, they pray. All the people, all the dying-in-the-same-way people, the doctors, nurses, husbands and children holding vigil around my mother, prayed that day in the hospital. A priest started saying the rosary, and a round little man, still in his mail carrier's uniform, put a pair of rosary beads into my mother's hands. Sing-song voices reciting the Hail Mary, voices filled with the possibility of a miracle, rose up together as if this powerful tool would be enough to change the course of my mother's fate.

That was the last time I beseeched God to hear me because I prayed that He would let my mother live, and she died anyway.

Anna O'Malley Catalina's wake was my first exposure to the rituals associated with death. I learned that family and friends emerge from the woodwork to pay their respects, and that old gripes dissolve because death erases the blackboard of life. My mother's family did not come to her funeral. They were, on the whole, a strange lot, and for the most part stayed away in life and in death. Her own mother had died when she was a child, leaving her to be raised by a father who found consolation in a bottle of whiskey.

I have a vague recollection of my grandfather O'Malley. He would visit us in Fall River and sleep over. He stayed because most times he was too drunk to drive home. Grandpa O'Malley was a harmless alcoholic, not one to get violent or aggressive; he just drank until his pain was gone. One morning he didn't wake up. He had died in his sleep on our couch.

When my cancer was diagnosed, one of the questions asked concerned family members and their current status: alive or dead. If dead, the questionnaire wanted to know how each of these individuals who made up the fabric of my genealogy had died. Where to begin? Neither of my parents had siblings. I could not reach to absent sisters or brothers for answers. My point of reference was grandparents, and so I filled in the blanks with Joseph Catalina: heart attack; Rose Grimaldi Catalina: complications from a broken hip; Edward O'Malley: complications brought on by alcohol. When I got to Rita O'Malley I put the pen down.

My mother had told me she remembered her mother getting very thin and that there were dark circles under her eyes. She slept a lot, my mother said, and she could recall climbing up next to her, putting her ear on her chest and listening to her heartbeat. This was in the late forties, just after the war, when other people were trying to get their lives back together, and my grandfather was a young man with a little girl and a dead wife.

I resumed writing on the form. Rita O'Malley: breast cancer. Anna O'Malley Catalina: breast cancer.

The stark realization that my mother's mother had died from the beast sealed my fate. Nothing could change my mind about my destiny, nothing until Whales Market, nothing short of a living nightmare.

Victor Catalina chose to have his wife, my mother, laid out in an open casket at McBride's Funeral Home near the wharf in Gloucester. The rosary beads from the hospital were wrapped around her folded hands. The bruised color was gone, replaced by a coat of flesh-colored makeup. In life, my mother wore only pale shades of lipstick, and despite whispers of how well she was done up, her death pose looked artificial.

People sat in folding chairs arranged in rows, as if an intimate performance had been scheduled for these special guests. As visitors filed into the room with my mother's coffin center stage, they had to pass a separate row of chairs set out for immediate family. We had assigned seats in order, it seemed, of how deep our sorrow was or how close our connection to Anna O'Malley Catalina.

Claire Laskey sat next to her son Peter. He was the row's first bookend, the person designated *loved her but not enough to be at the other end.* Next to Claire sat Grandma Rose, Grandpa Joe, my brother Martin, myself and at the end of the row, Victor Catalina. There was a lot of kissing, hand shaking, hard hugs and whispers in our ears. Assorted stale odors emanated from the line of mourners, and when they leaned down into our faces, we could smell rotting lunch left on their teeth or the last glass of stout swigged before coming to pay their respects.

My father was unfeeling to all these intrusions on his senses. He was the other bookend not holding anything up. His body leaned forward, arched towards the casket, turned away from the steady stream of visitors. Every so often he would rise from his seat and walk over to where my mother rested. Closer and closer he would edge himself towards his dead wife, until he stood at her feet, his arms slung low on his hips with hands clasped tight together.

Mourners paid their respects two by two, on the dark blue upholstered kneeler placed mid-coffin. Despite the perfect viewing position, most people looked down, crossed themselves, and moved on. Others wiped tears from their eyes and looked from my mother to my father. He did not acknowledge anyone. He was alone in a crowded room that smelled of gladiolas and old ladies' perfume.

Grandma Rose got up several times from her place in our neat little row to stand next to her Victor. She acted as a barrier between my father and the never-ending stream of visitors. She kissed cheeks, held hands, gave hugs and thanked each one in turn, all the while allowing her son to keep his last silent watch over Anna O'Malley Catalina.

Two years and a few months later, Claire Laskey and Victor married. Claire would welcome her new life and family, following through on her promise to my mother. Both she and Victor came to Cape Ann to reclaim us. Martin accepted Claire, even called her Mom, but, no surprise, I was still unable to identify her as anyone but my mother's best friend. As for returning to Fall River in what would be the beginning of my senior year in high school, I said no. All the reasons that I had not wanted to leave Fall River—my home, entering high school, my friends and my life with the people I loved—had become the same reasons that I could not now leave Gloucester. My home with my grandparents, my senior year of high school, my friends, especially Kathy Emerald, and my new life; yes, I'd miss Marty, but he'd be fine, I knew that.

My grandparents told me not to be angry at my father for marrying Claire, that their marriage in no way meant he cared less for my mother, and that his devotion to his Anna lasted beyond the day she died.

EIGHT

Kathy came to my mother's wake. She stood behind my chair in the designated row and put her hands on my shoulders. She stood there for all the hours that we sat, only changing her stance to take a greeting extended in her direction. A few people remembered her from our visit in August and seemed relieved to be able to share conversation with her. The next morning at the funeral, Kathy stayed close. She sat next to me in the family pew, oblivious to any rules of etiquette or protocol. I didn't cry, not once, and in that respect we were the same, our feelings always in check.

When the mourners gathered at the cemetery, Kathy made sure she had my hand in hers. Claire and Peter stood together off to the side, my mother's friend visibly undone by the finality of the burial. Martin and our grandparents pressed themselves close to the casket, but not as close as Victor. He moved the chair set out for him under the funeral awning almost into the hole overlapped with strips of fake grass. No one stopped him, no one said, "Mr. Catalina you need to get back into the row." He slipped his fingers around one of the casket's handles, and stared out onto the mound of baby roses sprayed across the polished lid. For anyone watching there was no doubt about the depth of his loss. I couldn't look at my father, couldn't look in that direction at all. The entire service lasted about thirty minutes, and for its entirety I put my head on Kathy's shoulder and closed my eyes.

Like the ballast of a ship, Kathy kept me afloat. Watching her yesterday, I saw that nothing had changed. Kathy was still keeping me from sinking.

"I'm not going into Rockport to my mother's," she said. "Jack will understand if I take you directly home."

"I'll call him when I get in," I said, zipping my jacket and searching my bag for something to cover my hands. Down at the bottom, turned inside out, was a bright pink pair of child-size, stretch-knit gloves, Annalise's contribution to my Tuesday supplies. After a few false starts, my hands found the slots to the yarn fingers, and I used my teeth to pull each glove past the center of my palms.

"Just drop me off at the bottom of the hill close to the main road," I said, attempting to manipulate a pink thumb against my molars. "I'll walk the rest of the way."

"Do you think you can walk up the hill to your house?" Kathy asked. "This storm is wicked, I don't know if I can just drop you off. I'm going to try to make the hill. We'll see how far I get and then decide."

"You're the best, Kath," I said. "We'll laugh about this some day."

"Another tale for our memoirs," she added, sounding relieved that we had only a short distance more to go. Once we crossed the bridge we didn't see another vehicle except for snowplows. We passed Whales Market, and I could see the lights on inside. There were no cars in the parking lot, only a few food carts abandoned helter-skelter in the snow. I could have asked Kathy to stop, but I didn't want her to be part of my plan or privy to my idea. Celebrating all the occasions I would miss after I died was still paramount in my mind. Annalise's fifth birthday was going to be the party of all parties. Yesterday, I never thought about how Annalise would feel, or Jack, or the boys. The party was less and less about my daughter and my family, and more and more about me.

I turned my head as we slowly rolled past Whales. I knew Ruby Desmond was in there and would still be there when I went back.

"I'll call you later to see how you're doing," Kathy said.

"Honestly, Kath, it is such a relief to know that no one will be home. I will probably go straight to bed," I said. "Give me a quick call when you get home and then I'll see you tomorrow for Annalise's party."

Kathy nodded okay and began her ascent up the hill to my house. I knew the pickup truck would be able to make the climb later on, but now I wasn't sure about Kathy's van.

We got about three quarters of the way up when Kathy conceded to let me out and walk the rest of the way.

"Look," I said, "you can sit here for the two minutes it will take me to get up to the house. I'll flash the lights when I get in and then you can leave." I leaned over the car console and kissed her on the cheek. "Don't worry, I'll be fine," I said.

I opened the door and slid off the seat. The snow was up to my knees and the wind twisted around me, distorting familiar shapes and landmarks. The outline of the roof was still visible and the porch light was on. It took longer than a few minutes to reach the house and get inside. Kathy sat waiting with the car running, exhaust billowing out around its elephant shape.

When I got to the garage, I collapsed. One hot pink hand reached for a shovel propped against the door. My other hand was splayed against the cedar shingles, and with slow, deliberate movements I reached for the keypad. I punched in the code, and the garage door opened. I stumbled into its cold space and found the light switch to signal Kathy. Having done that, I hit the button to drop the door back down and then sank to my knees.

A picture of people kissing the tarmac after returning home from some perilous journey flashed into my mind, which set the whole praying thing into motion again. Still on my knees I managed to pull open the storm and inside doors to the house. As the inner one swung back, I fell forward onto my stomach, hospital bag flying over my head. Yellow Dog was sitting in the mudroom, tail wagging and banging against the brick floor. He didn't bark.

"Good boy," I muttered, my face pressed into the welcome mat.

It took several minutes to get the strength to roll over. The phone was going to ring. Kathy would be calling. Once I was on my back, Yellow Dog licked my face. Ordinarily I would balk at this canine expression of love, but yesterday I needed that splash of saliva to help pull myself together. I was up on all fours when the phone rang. Moving like a toddler, I crawled to the wall-phone. I reached up with both arms and pulled the receiver down onto the floor.

"Hud, are you okay?" It was Kathy.

"I'm good," I said. "Just having a little trouble getting to the phone. I'm exhausted. I need to rest. Do me a favor and call Jack. Tell him I'm going to bed and I'll call him later." I meant the part about being tired, but I didn't think I could make it to bed. My plan was to stay on the floor until I felt better. The trip to Whales Market was going to be delayed.

Yellow Dog seemed to grin at me, a wet, full-toothed dog smile. I patted his back and looked around for something soft to put my head on. The nearest thing was his bed.

"Okay, boy, you and I are going to share that warm space," I said, sliding myself over to the big corduroy cushion in the corner of the room. The phone in my lap traveled with me. The dog was eager for attention and found my proximity to him alluring. He continued to lick my face as I edged my way onto his large pillow and curled myself into a fetal position.

"I'm so tired," I said to the dog. He looked down at me with what could only be described as compassion, and if a dog could shrug, he did. Then Yellow Dog climbed up onto his bed, spun around a few times, and finally settled with a distinct *plop* next to me. He laid his big head across my upper body and gave out a low sigh.

"Good boy," I said, and we both fell asleep.

In that crossover between deep sleep and waking is a place where dreams collide with reality. I closed my eyes and entered through those portals and found myself standing outside what I guessed was my house. It was a different color and shape, but I knew it was Ten Nettles Cove. A tree had fallen onto the roof, creating a huge gash that exposed the rooms inside. Jack and the boys were trying to fix the damage. Each of them had a tool of some kind but seemed to be making minimal progress. Annalise was nowhere in sight, and I was carrying a plate of what I thought were cookies, but looked more like dog biscuits. No one seemed to notice me walking around the yard. I went up to Jack and asked him when the tree fell, and he ignored me, acting as if I wasn't there. This frustrated me so much that I sat in front of his toolbox, blocking it from him, and kept talking. Off in the distance I could hear the jingle of an ice-cream truck's bell. The children heard it too, dropped their hammers and ran towards the sound. Jack called after them, telling the boys to come back, but they kept running towards the ringing.

When Jack gave up on getting his helpers to return, he reached into his toolbox. His hand went through me like in a magic trick. I flung the plate I was holding into the air and woke up.

The ringing in the dream was real, except it was the telephone and not an ice-cream truck. My eyes were wide open, and between the phone's rings I could hear the soft snoring sounds of the dog.

"Hello ..."

"Hud?" It was Jack. "Thank God, this is the third time I called."

"I guess I was sleeping," I said. "Sorry to make you worry."

"Kathy said you were going to bed, but I needed to hear your voice," he said, and I thought about my dream, how he couldn't hear my voice and how I was invisible.

"Don't worry about me. Yellow Dog is looking after me. We'll be okay until you get here tomorrow," I said. "Honest, Jack, it's okay. I'm fine."

"I don't know, Hud. Something has me feeling very uneasy. I can't put my finger on it, but I just have this sense that ..."

His voice trailed off as if he needed to stop that thought from becoming a reality. "Go back to sleep, I'll talk to you later," he said. "I love you."

"And you," I said.

The dog and I were enveloped in darkness. Night had settled in. My plan seemed remote and improbable at that moment. Lying in the black shadows filling the mudroom, I briefly considered abandoning my trip to Whales. I needed to check the time and take my next dose of medication. The walk up the hill had taken its toll, and I did not want to move. The dog must have sensed my indecision because he made a small *ruff-ruff* noise in the back of his throat.

"Okay, boy," I said. "Let's get a light on." When we reached the kitchen, I turned on the small desk lamp next to the door and opened the refrigerator. Perched on the middle shelf of the freezer sat Annalise's cupcakes. Each hardened confection peered at me through a pale blue zip-lock bag. I took the four dozen little cakes out and placed them on the counter. Once they were in front of me, my plan to go to Whales was restored.

First things first, I thought, and went back into the mudroom to get my hospital bag. For the second time, I rummaged through it, this time looking for my medication. I lined up each bottle like a toy soldier on a butcher-block battlefield. It was a little past seven, and I calculated no meds before eight. A loud churning sound came from my stomach. I didn't know if I was hungry or if another eruption was brewing. My anti-emetic prescription had fallen over in the line-up, and I took this as an omen that I shouldn't wait until I got back from

Whales to take it with the others.

There was some tea left in the pot from the morning. I poured myself a cup and put it in the microwave. While it was heating, I went out to start the truck. The keys were on a hook next to the garage door, which I opened just enough to let out the exhaust and the dog. The driver's seat of the truck was as frigid and stiff as Annalise's cupcakes. I climbed in and tried to put the key into the ignition. My sleeves were pulled down around my hands, but my fingers were cold and uncooperative. Once I managed to make my hands work, I started pumping the gas. In cold weather, the old pick-up will usually cough and choke before starting. I worked the pedal with my right foot as best I could. Again I thought about praying, but for me, it was too many times in one day. Instead I let luck take the credit for the engine turning on the first try.

I returned to the kitchen and took a few swallows of tea with my one pill. There was no time to press my cold hands against the hot mug because the dog was scratching to come in, and I had given myself less than an hour to do a round trip to Whales. If I was going to do this crazy thing, I had to leave.

Yellow Dog bolted past me as I opened the inside door. He shook himself off, sending a wet spray of fur and snow in all directions. I couldn't move fast enough to avoid his splatter, and it didn't matter anyway; my jeans were still damp from my walk through the snow.

I went back into the house and into my bedroom. Heaviness hung in the corners even with the lights on. As I moved towards the closet, I tripped over a shoe on the floor. Looking down, I realized it was the same one responsible for the shattered mirror. What was it Kathy had been trying to tell me in the morning? She said that I was asking too much of Jack and the kids. I surveyed the aftermath of my transgression and silently agreed with her.

In my dream, the tree had fallen across the bed in our room. It had disrupted the peace usually found there and had struck a fatal blow. I looked around and felt the eerie memory. Changing my jeans was not possible. I didn't have the strength. Every fiber of my being was shaken. A wave of nausea came and went, I hesitated, and then, holding onto the end of the bed, turned and went back out to the mudroom.

I found an old ski jacket, put it on, and stuck my wallet in its zippered breast pocket. On my head I pulled down a wool hat that Grandma Rose had made for Jack and put on a pair of gloves and rubber boots that belonged to the boys. If this was my fashion statement, there would be no one to witness it, except maybe for Ruby Desmond when I got to Whales Market.

"Go lie down, boy," I said to the dog. "I'll be back in thirty minutes. Be good while I'm gone." I put the truck into reverse and backed out into the storm.

PART II

Heroes are the most unassuming, and the most
improbable of individuals.

NINE

I looked out the rearview mirror into a wall of white fury. Even with the high beams on, there was no chance of seeing anything in front of me. The door to the garage came down with a soft *wham* against a layer of snow. Thick, blinding precipitation masked the truck's windows, as if the forces of nature were taking me hostage.

I nosed the pickup down the hill, away from the house. The truck and I were in motion, and somehow the old Chevy seemed to drive itself towards Whales. So many trips to the market over the years had conditioned it to take a left off Nettles Cove onto the main road, stop at one light and then take a right into the parking lot. Since mine was the only vehicle in sight, it didn't seem to matter where or even how I parked. There was only one grocery cart left, of the few I'd seen earlier when I drove by with Kathy. I pulled in next to the sole cart to shorten my reach for it.

A flood of anxiety washed over me, causing palpitations and shortness of breath. I had misjudged the timing of my medication, and I would continue to pay the price. My head bowed onto the steering wheel as I down-shifted and pulled the hand brake up. A familiar seasick sensation settled over me. One pill had *not* been enough.

Through the windshield I saw a shadow, eclipse-like, slowly come into view and disappear again, perhaps a person or perhaps my imagination. I curled my fingers around the handle and swung the door open. There was a loud clunk as it hit the grocery cart. Planting one foot on the ground, I was able to lean onto the cart, grip the handle and steady myself.

A surge of toxins pushed its way up my esophagus. My head rolled like a rag doll, and to stay anchored I squatted down, arms raised overhead. Jack's too-large snow hat had pinned itself uncomfortably over my left ear. Huge flakes of snow pelted my naked skull. Lifting one shoulder, I attempted to coax the hat back into place.

A pair of bulbous, heavy-duty boots appeared in my line of vision. The laces were double knotted, and the feet belonged to Willy Wu. Willy bagged groceries for Whales and also collected the carts. His full name was William Woodrow Wulinsky, but somewhere in the mix he became Willy Wu. Maybe the Wu came from unkind kids, or maybe it was Willy who found a shortcut through the Ws and re-christened himself.

The Wulinskys had lived a few blocks from my grandparents with five other children besides Willy. He was number three in that family's birth order, and the only one not born full-term without complications. Willy Wulinsky's entry on New Year's Day, twenty-nine years ago, came prematurely, with barely enough time to reach the local hospital. That Willy survived his first near collision with death, only minutes into his life, was a miracle.

My grandmother referred to Willy as Mrs. Wulinsky's *special child*; this explained everything to Grandma Rose, but nothing to me. He is different, she would say. Mrs. Wulinsky and Grandma Rose believed Willy's birth was a gift from God. Since I had given up on God when my mother died, I thought their faith was remarkable.

Willy was about five when I moved to Gloucester and was as much a part of the Catalina household as my brother and myself. Mrs. Wulinsky worked for my grandparents. She did all the baking and made an array of desserts that kept customers coming back day after day. Her pies were unmatched fruit concoctions piled high under melt-in-your-mouth crust. A food critic from the *Globe* summered on Cape Ann and often mentioned the Catalina Bistro when writing about the best local fare. Mrs. Wulinsky's desserts were described at length, leaving readers yearning for a baked crust that the writer mistakenly thought had become a lost art.

Willy Wu would come to work with his mother and sit on the floor between the commercial refrigerator and the double sink. He played an endless game of his own devising with three empty tomato cans, an array of salt and peppershakers and a wooden spoon. From his vantage point, the view was of feet, ankles and knees. Whenever he looked up from his game, it was into a sea of moving limbs, unshaven calves, olive oil–stained khakis or half-rolled hose cinched under dimpled kneecaps.

Sometimes I would catch my brother sitting next to Mrs. Wulinsky's son and see how intently he watched Willy Wu's small hands moving the cans, conducting the orchestra of pepper and salt with his spoon raised high over his head. He seemed unaware of our presence, avoiding eye contact and resistant to affection. Socially, Willy was a loner, always preoccupied within his own world. When Willy got tired he hummed, sometimes for hours. Wrapped secure with his arms around his knees, Willy Wulinsky would rock and hum until he fell asleep.

Yesterday Willy Wu appeared oblivious of those memories. He had come out into the blizzard a giant Big Foot, a mythical beast trying to scare a woman with breast cancer or simply to retrieve my food cart because that was his job, and nothing else mattered. Willy was inflexible and I was expendable.

My mind started to play tricks on me and suddenly Willy Wu was small, as little as my Annalise. I remembered that both he and Annalise were Capricorns. It is so bizarre, the parade of thoughts that jig through your head when you are unwell. Someone told me once that Capricorns are old souls, people who have, if you believe in reincarnation, lived many previous lives. They have innate wisdom. I accepted that about my daughter, and of Willy Wu.

Annalise is unique, not, like Willy, a child of medical circumstance, but unusual because she has a *knowing* that only someone who has lived many lifetimes could have. Perhaps Willy Wu has the same gift, but it is locked inside, past-life wisdom swirling and twirling in the dark corridors of his cerebral space. Yesterday I would have said no to the possibility of Willy's profound insight, but today I know better.

Willy tugged on my cart and I threw up again. This time my hat tumbled off my head and was blown away in slow motion. I bleated like an old goat while Willy grunted and talked to himself. He took hold of the cart from its opposite end, dug his large fingers into its rungs and hauled it away. My hands were jerked free of the handle by the force of his grip. I placed them on my naked scalp, elbows pressed together in front of my nose. The wind whipped at me, I bent my head and walked into the storm for the second time.

Ruby Desmond was at the door when Willy and I paraded in. Her white hair was pulled back tight, forming hundreds of ridges on the top of her head. The profusion of hairs that refused to lie flat rose in a wispy halo around her black face and the rest fell down to the middle of her spine in a braid.

Ruby was well into her eighties with only a few wrinkles around her eyes, but their defined presence suggested the possibility of secrets, the kind that lie deep below the surface.

"Honey, what's you doing out in this weather?" she asked me. Her voice held a hint of her southern roots. "This here storm is bad. You shouldn't be out. Turn around and get yourself back home." Ruby pointed to the door.

I hesitated before answering. Still focused on my birthday party mission, still intent on following through, I failed to recognize I was at a crossroad. I failed to see the option of turning around on my green camouflage boots and going back home where life was safe and insulated.

Willy didn't move. Now that all the carts were inside, he seemed unsure what to do next.

"Child, line those wagons up good and then get a bag of salt to put on the ice outside the door." She emphasized her words to Willy with a little wave of her fingers. "Remember, Willy, I called your Mamma and told her you'd be sleeping upstairs tonight."

Ruby moved over to the window, took hold of her apron, and with one corner rubbed a clear circle to look out. Cupping her hands like a wide-angle lens, she pressed them into the glass around the clear space. The frame of her palms was a perfect fit for her face.

"Ruby ..."

Still short of breath and feeling nauseous, my voice came out pinched. She turned her head slightly as if cocking her ear to hear me better. Her feet and legs were spread, giving her broad body the power to go head first into the storm.

"I need to get some decorations for Annalise's birthday party."

Ruby Desmond shook her head as she continued to survey the almost-empty parking lot. "What you want will be here tomorrow," she said. "Go on and get yourself back in your truck and go home."

"No, Ruby," I said. "It'll take only a few minutes." I left her looking out the window and headed for the baking supplies in aisle three.

Willy glanced over at me as I patted Ruby on the arm, promising to be quick. His expression seemed curious, and when I caught his eye, he looked away. He had taken my grocery wagon and perhaps he had a fleeting thought of giving it back to me.

Aisle three had everything anyone needed to bake, fry or frost. Mid-way into the row were candles and decorations, a little further down doilies, crepe paper and balloons. I wanted to browse, but I had to keep my promise to Ruby. She had a display of cake pans next to the flour and sugar. They were on sale. I opened the front pouch of my jacket and shoved four pans inside. Into my side pockets I stuffed candles, wax replicas related to dance, sports, graduation and special events. Birthday numbers, zero through nine, went into my breast pockets, along with some extra zeros for double-digit celebrations.

Willy Woodrow Wulinsky came down the aisle carrying a bag of ice salt. He stopped for a few seconds and watched me plopping candle after candle into my jacket.

"Do you like this one, Willy?" I had a gymnast, hands down, feet poised upward with a wick daintily peeking out of one foot.

He looked at me but made no comment.

"Do you like it?" I held up the wax figure again. "I know Annalise will like it," I said. "This is her fifth birthday. We're going to have a party for her tomorrow. Will you come, Willy?" I asked him. "Come to the party for Annalise?"

He started to turn away from me and then looked back.

"Willy Wu works!" he answered and moved down the aisle.

"When you get off work tomorrow, when you finish, Willy, please come," I said this to his back. He didn't answer. The bag of salt made a fingernails-on-the-blackboard sound as he dragged it across the floor. Willy put one of his fingers in his ear and I laughed to myself.

Ruby had come away from the window to stand at the end of aisle three. I felt her watching me but didn't look up. She was going to ask questions; it was coming, I knew.

"Hudson, you are acting real strange tonight," Ruby said. "What's got into you, honey?"

My stomach ached and I could feel pain soaking into my limbs. The pat replies I had rehearsed since this morning were now forgotten. I gave her a sidelong glance, and she stared back at me unflinching. Her hands graced her ample hips, long, dark fingers poised in question.

"This is something I've got to do, Ruby," I said. "Something I've been thinking about all day." I sat down on the floor to go through the paper plates. "I know it's beyond reason," I continued, "but I had to be here tonight, not tomorrow."

Ruby wiped her hands on her apron and came over to me.

"The Lord puts us where we're supposed to be, honey," she said and lowered her bulky frame down onto the linoleum. "Tell me what it is you need, child, and together we'll get it done."

"Thank you," I said.

"Hush," Ruby replied, pulling out several packages of party napkins, "no thanks needed."

We sat side by side not speaking. The only sound was Willy Wu wrestling with the task of melting ice. My pile of decorations had grown and my pockets were full.

"It's none of my business, Hudson, but what you going to do with all this party stuff?" she said, her face a shadow in the coarse, overhead lighting.

My plan had not included disclosure, but Ruby was confessional close, and there would be no absolution until I told her the whole truth.

"I'm dying, Ruby," I said. "This is the last of Annalise's birthdays that I'll be able to celebrate." My voice cracked, not from tears, but from the effort it took to mentally bypass the level of pain arising in my body. "I need to do this," I drew my hand across the stack of party supplies, "for me."

"I died once," Ruby said. She put down the cellophane-wrapped packets and lifted her left arm. A small bracelet dangled from her wrist.

"Can you read this?" she asked me.

The muscles in my legs quivered and a slow chill ran along my spine as I pushed my face in close to the inscription. Across its silver face was written 2nd Lt. Abraham L. Desmond, USMC 1 May 67 Laos. I looked up at Ruby, and I could see how her eyes had gone wet with sorrow.

"I'm so sorry, Ruby," I said.

Abraham Lincoln Desmond was Ruby's son. There were stories about him, the way there are tales about people in a small town. In the past I hadn't cared much about what folk had to say, but I was wrong, I should have listened, should have paid attention. Ruby's son was missing in action in Vietnam and, despite the military declaring that there were no soldiers left behind, Abe had never been found.

"There's all kinds of dying, honey," she said. "The way I see it, I had two choices. Either give up hope and let death take my boy, or keep hope alive by waiting for him with the lights on and Whales Market open twenty-four hours a day, seven days a week."

There was a long silence between us. Ruby took my hand and placed it between both of hers.

"A Mamma has got to do what a Mamma has to do," she said. This I took as her blessing and approval for buying out her party inventory.

Willy had slipped between us unheard. The look on his face told me he had been listening, a quiet spectator to our revelations. How much did Willy understand? I looked at him and then back at Ruby.

"Willy here, he knows about Abe," Ruby said as if reading my mind. "Isn't that right, Willy?"

He stood awkwardly. Both of us looked at him and waited for an answer. One of his hands opened and closed repeatedly, while the other took his eyeglasses off and put them back on, on and off. Ruby smiled at him.

"There's no need to be nervous," she said with a calm voice. "We're your friends, Ruby and Hudson, and friends talk together like we're doing right now. So leave your glasses be, child, and tell Hudson about Abe."

Willy still didn't answer. His mouth moved and his tongue brushed the air, but no words came out. I saw how he strained to reply, how, I thought, the words, instead of creating a sentence, got caught in a net of confusion. He replaced his glasses for about the fifth or sixth time, gave us a lopsided grin and took off in a lumbering run.

TEN

Ruby didn't seem surprised that he had left so suddenly. She was chuckling to herself, muttering "that boy," over and over.

"Where did he go?" I asked her. "Did I scare him away?"

"No, child," Ruby answered. "That boy has gone upstairs to get some photographs of my Abe. I know Willy like he was my own." She paused and laid out a few rows of napkins so I could see each one. "If he can't tell you what's on his mind, then he'll show you. Sometimes that's much easier than trying to get the words to come out in an arrangement that makes sense."

I was remembering again the Willy Wu of my childhood. "His mother worked for my grandparents years ago, and I remember him as a little boy conducting kitchen props under the restaurant's work table."

"Ah, yes," Ruby said as if she had also borne witness to the exact memory.

Her love for Willy showed, and he was, admittedly, her favorite among the young people that worked for her. Willy Wu was one of five employees that counted on Whales Market for a paycheck. She chose to give them a clean environment to be productive and happy. Ruby considered them *Lambs of the Lord*, taken from her firm belief in the Bible. In the years after her Abe was reported missing, Ruby struggled to find a good reason to live. She sought guidance in her deep religious roots, and from that came the first of Ruby's *lambs*.

Sometimes when the weather was too hot or too cold, or bad like yesterday, she would alert the families or the group home in town and have her *lambs* stay overnight. There was a dormitory-like room arranged upstairs where they had their own bed and space. Ruby had become adopted family, and for some their only family.

Willy began working for Whales about seven years ago. He wasn't like the others, she said. William Woodrow Wulinsky was special. I wondered if Ruby and Grandma Rose had ever discussed this fact together.

He could follow directions to the letter, she explained with pride, and he seemed to enjoy his tasks. There was never a problem with absence. Willy arrived punctually at seven a.m., walking from his mother's house, about a quarter of a mile away, and always departed Whales on the dot of three, retracing his exact route reversed.

I told her about Annalise and my old soul theory, and how I was sure that Willy, too, must be very wise. Ruby agreed and said she wasn't sure why, only that Willy's ability to find expression in music and color had been, for her, like the opening of a window painted shut.

"He is perceptive," she continued. "Some people think folk like Willy lack empathy, but I declare that to be false. Willy is a great mimic. If you are happy, he'll clap and smile. If you're angry, he'll put his hands over his ears, and if you're sad, he'll reach into his pocket and pull out his handkerchief. Willy doesn't follow any profile or stereotype. He knows what he needs to do. He didn't learn it in school or in a book, he just knows."

Perhaps his family is part of the reason. I offered more possibilities to Ruby. I remember Mrs. Wulinsky always treated Willy with fairness and that he was never put outside the circle of his siblings or peers. In a house with five children, everyone had chores to do, Willy included. If he needed to be scolded, she doled out the same penance to him as she did to the others.

Ruby made a clucking sound with her lips that drew my attention away from our conversation and onto the floor. She had made rows and rows of plates, napkins and cups while we were talking. Peacock shades of primary colors were spread like a fanned tail on the worn tiles.

"Oh, Ruby," I said, "I want one of every color." She seemed pleased, gave a little cluck again and picked one from each row.

"I'm going to take these over to the check-out, honey," she said. "Would you like some tea? I'm going to brew a pot for us."

"Thank you, but no, Ruby," I said. "I promised you I'd be quick, and I've already taken up so much of your time."

"Child, have you looked outside lately? There isn't anything going on out there, or in here, that we can't stop for tea."

"Okay, I'll have a cup with you, but first may I please use your restroom?" Sharp stings of pain came as I tried to get up. My left leg was asleep and I had to hold onto the cake mix shelf to shake it out. Needle and pinpricks prevented me from putting weight on my foot. I didn't have the strength to hop, so I waited, propped against the chocolate and marble cakes, until the feeling returned. Once I could move, the weight of my jacket became apparent. Both of my shoulders caved inward from the load in my pockets. If I had been in better humor, I would have found my predicament amusing, but I was still carrying some of the darkness of the day and could only smile to myself over what I must look like.

The restroom was down aisle five at the back of the store. Ruby busied herself with making tea, and Willy was still upstairs. Small packets of medicinal travel supplies lined the back wall, as well as men's birth control and ladies' feminine hygiene supplies. This mixed marriage of needs acted as a backdrop to an otherwise dreary corner. I stopped to steady myself and wondered if an over-the-counter analgesic would dent my discomfort. The only way to know was to try. Six mini-sealed bags of minor relief went into the pocket with my wallet and the buy-two-for-one pans.

When the door to the bathroom closed behind me, I sank onto the toilet and put my head between my knees. I kept this pose for several minutes, trying to regain some composure. The room was small and immaculate. On the back of the door hung a bulletin board with colorful tacks clustered in one corner. Assorted snippets of wisdom hung from its cork surface, each one presumably donated by former restroom occupants. A yellowed piece of paper had "*Love is the answer*" scrawled across it in blue ink. Another one asked that we forgive our enemies, and someone had hand-written above it *but we should not sleep with them.*

Disposable cups were stacked neatly against a tall plastic container of toilet tissue. Hand embroidered doilies rested beneath each one, adding dignity to the most banal of life's necessities. I twisted myself on the commode and filled a cup with water. The packets were difficult to open. After several tries, I managed to free four tablets and stuff them into my mouth. The water felt good going down.

I took a few deep breaths and continued to look around at my surroundings. The room was windowless. An overhead fan droned in a loud, monotonous hum. Its blades cut the air with swift slaps and sent off enough breeze to make me shiver. A huge plastic sunflower was the only wall decoration next to the sink. Inside the petals, where the brown center should be, was a clock. It was twenty minutes after nine. I groaned thinking about my medication. Unwrapping two more packets, I swallowed four additional pills. As I tossed the cup into the small trash receptacle, the market's entrance buzzer sounded. At first I thought that Ruby had gone out and come back in again, but then I heard a male voice that clearly was not Willy Wu's.

There was a garbled exchange of words that slowly escalated to a steady, high pitch. I straightened up and moved towards the door to listen. Something told me to be quiet. Slowly I opened the door a crack. I had a clear line of vision to the cash register from my position.

Ruby was in full view with arms crossed against her large chest. The set of her lips was one solid line. The man across the counter moved in and out of my sight, and I tried to get a fix on who he was and why he was angry. A dark hood covered his head, pulled low to shroud his eyes, leaving only a sharp nose and chin for identification. From the length of aisle five, I wasn't close enough to discern who it could be. Each time the figure moved back into sight, something chrome-like and shiny flapped against his hip. I pressed my face against the inside molding of the door and one eye between the opening.

"Take your cigarettes, boy," Ruby said in a stern voice. "Take them and get out of my store. If you got no money, you got no beer coming to you. I'll give you the cigarettes in good faith but nothing else without money." She tucked her arms in tighter to her chest and glared in stubborn defiance at her customer.

The silver objects hanging off the man's belt rattled. Handcuffs! Yes, I bent my forehead deeper into the door's edge, that's what they were: *handcuffs*. Gloved fingers reached over the glass case filled with penny candy and snatched the cigarettes from Ruby.

"Black bitch," the words came off the intruder's lips harsh and bitter. He turned and left. The buzzer went off again. This time the echo of its sound sent fear through me. I closed the door and leaned on the knob with both hands.

Who was that?

There was a nagging, familiar tone to his voice. Well, I said to myself, at least he's gone. I opened the door feeling a little better and anxious for a cup of tea. The cargo in my pockets banged together as I walked up to the front of the store. When I reached the register, I placed some candles on the counter.

"Did you hear that white trash calling me names?" Ruby asked. "He's got some nerve coming in here without money and expecting me to just give him beer and cigarettes." She was inside a small room behind the checkout. I stuck my head in; it was such a contrast to the store. Daffodils in bouquets of assorted sizes ran the perimeter of the room, their imprinted wallpaper's repetition never tiring of heralding spring. Yellow seat cushions were tied on four wooden chairs at a small table, and the yellow theme persisted on the cabinets and scatter rugs. Ruby laid out a tablecloth, and onto that she placed a mug and two delicate porcelain teacups. A television was positioned catty-corner to the eating area, turned just enough to allow diners to eat without being distracted by soap operas, recent crime or politics.

"I heard him," I said. "Who was it?"

"Buddy Baker," she answered, a look of disgust on her face. "That boy was raised by the devil himself and has been nothing but trouble his whole life. I've tried to be kind to him, even tonight. I gave him a pack of cigarettes." She laid a flowered plate of cookies on the table next to the cups. "But it don't matter none, he will never be grateful, he just goes on acting like a damn fool."

I knew Buddy Baker. What Ruby Desmond was saying about him was the truth. He had been one of my students at the high school several years ago. Buddy and I had spent many afternoons of detention together. This wasn't good; all the red flags were flapping.

"It's a good thing he didn't see me," I said. "I am not one of his favorite people."

"Don't matter, child," she said. "Buddy's got no friends around here, unless you count the low-lifes he hangs around with on the pier."

The teakettle whistled and acted as a distraction to calm Ruby's agitation. "Set yourself down, Hudson, and let's not think about that boy anymore."

But think about him I did, I couldn't help myself. Memories of Buddy squirmed out of my subconscious, took precedence over what I was doing, my purpose at Whales Market. Memories real or imagined were suddenly Technicolor.

Willy came around the corner, his face flushed. Perspiration glowed on his forehead and temples.

"Hey, Willy," I said, trying to ignore my mental montage. "Where have you been hiding?" He put out his right hand to me and dropped a double photo frame in my lap. "What have you got here?" I asked him.

"Abe," he said.

Ruby smiled and gave me a nod that said she'd been right about Willy. I spread the frame open. Looking back at me was a young man in a cap and gown, and the same young man in Marine dress blues. It struck me that he had his mother's eyes. They held your attention, even in a photograph. In the first picture, he had his arm around Ruby, who was also dressed in a cap and gown, both of them smiling wide and happy. The other photograph captured Abe alone as an officer with a serviceman's haircut and a military expression that flattened his mouth. Fresh out of Officer's Candidate School he showed pride and a youthful readiness to perform those duties required to defend his country.

"He's so handsome, Ruby," I said. She looked at me and dabbed the tears rolling down her cheek with the corner of her apron.

"That one there," she pointed to the graduation photo, "was taken the day he and I graduated from college." The rocking chair under her moved in a soothing fashion as she caught her breath and continued. "Abe made sure his Mamma got a GED certificate when he was in high school, and after that he said we were both going to college."

My teacup was half way to my lips when she told me about graduating from college. I felt my embarrassment begin to show.

"You can take that look off your face, child, not many people around here know or care that Ruby Desmond has a degree in business. It don't matter to me, I did it for my Abe, because he believed that women should be educated, no matter what their age, color or background."

"I'm sorry," I said. "I didn't mean to offend you."

"No," she said, "I'm not offended. I like you, Hudson, always have, and I don't think you've got a bone in your body that would deliberately set out to hurt anyone."

"Thank you, Ruby," I said. Willy had taken in our conversation and when we paused, he stepped over next to Ruby and put a finger on her shoulder, tapping it gently.

"What you want, child?" Ruby turned her head in his direction. He pointed to a bulge under his shirt. "What you got under there, Willy?" she asked.

Willy unrolled his shirt and pulled from its folds an American flag. The stars and stripes on its surface were over thirty years old. He handed the flag to Ruby and gave me a wooden box with brass hinges. Ruby held the flag to her heart, closed her eyes and rocked back and forth.

I brushed my fingers across the finely grained wood of the box before I opened it. Inside were four military decorations given to Abraham Lincoln Desmond, and a letter, yellowed by age, addressed to Ruby from the Secretary of Defense.

"These are all that this Mamma has left of that boy in the photograph." Ruby sighed and continued her rocking. "Some days are easier than others, but I never forget, I never close my eyes without thinking of him," she said.

I sat across from her at that tiny table, unable to conceive of her loss. I couldn't express proper sympathy by saying "I know how you feel," because all my children were alive and well. The question on my lips was, why did she carry on? But Ruby had already answered that; her faith. Ruby's faith was her glue. She held on because she never gave in, and I had, for my own reasons, given up.

ELEVEN

A silence formed around us as Ruby rocked, and I took sips of the hot liquid in my cup. Willy finally sat down. I gave him some cookies with tea. He leaned his arms onto the table, took the mug in both hands and looked away when I smiled at him.

"Thanks for bringing the pictures of Abe to show me," I said to Willy. His eyes were still averted, but I could sense he was pleased with himself. I studied his face, the faint hint of a grownup and the smooth skin of a boy. His features were nearly perfect, a finely chiseled nose with a slight fullness to the lips and chin. There was nothing there to suggest that there had been a mix-up at birth, a short stick or joker card pulled. Behind his glasses, which were thick and unforgiving, were deep blue pools: ocean eyes.

"How's your mother, Willy?" I asked. He looked at Ruby. The curved ends of her rocker squeaked every time she came forward, and the sound forced him and me to turn toward her. We were waiting for Ruby to speak again, waiting for her melancholy to lift.

The answer to my question, if he had one, never came. Willy wasn't thinking about home, his mother or anything except maybe how distant Ruby was at that moment.

Time no longer mattered to any of us. I wanted to get a few more things in aisle three, but since the incident with Buddy Baker, I had stopped worrying about my medication or the drive back to Nettles Cove. I dunked three cookies into my tea and savored the sweet taste as it entered my mouth. So many hours had passed since I threw my shoe into the mirror that I wondered, for the first time, if I had eaten anything at all until Ruby's cookies.

The sandwich that Kathy ate in the car was the last time a meal was even a thought, but I had to squeeze my eyes shut while she ate so it didn't count. Sitting at Ruby's, I satisfied my returned appetite with more cookies. Willy was not interested in food. He was so preoccupied with Ruby's flight of consciousness that I felt uncertain about what to do next. It was well after ten o'clock, and the packets of pills had worked a little on my pain. One part of me was still on a mission begun in the wee hours of the morning, but the larger part of me had separated from that need and wanted, instead, to linger with Willy and Ruby.

If she had died once, and I was dying now, then there was a bond between us, a connection that was as sure as the wind banging the clapboard shutters of Whales Market. She was more than just an acquaintance, more than just reliable Ruby. Willy, too, needed more exploration. All the days of passing over him, looking by him, absently thanking him for milk, eggs, cereal and dog food were congealed into a thick layer of another Willy Wu.

There were four more pills in my pocket. It had been an hour since I took the first eight. I laid the remaining packets on the table and began the process of opening the tiny packages. Willy shifted in his seat, observing my dilemma. I struggled, he watched for a while and without warning leaned behind my back and opened a drawer. With one motion devoid of clumsiness, he retrieved a pair of scissors and laid them in front of me. He looked down at his mug as I thanked him. I touched his arm, and a whole parade of words and sentences tumbled out of me as if I were the re-embodiment of Grandpa Joe talking to a corralled listener.

"When you were little, Willy," I told him, "you used to play with my brother and come to work with your mother at my grandparents' restaurant. Your mom baked delicious pies and cheesecakes. We would all get to lick the bowls with our fingers just before all the utensils went into the huge dishwasher. Do you recall those days, Willy?"

I asked this question along with several others, and all the while he looked off center of my eyes. He did not offer me any reminiscences in return. The past seemed to have no bearing on Willy's connection to the present.

"Willy can hear and understand all you're saying," Ruby broke in, "but he can't process his response back to you."

She put the flag in her apron pocket, along with Abe's pictures and medals, picked up her teacup and swallowed hard. Both Willy and I were relieved that Ruby had rejoined us. Her face was still puckered from her tears and the drain of an emotional plug that's been pulled. The worn surface of her apron had risen like fresh bread dough. She patted the temporary resting place for Abe's mementoes, and I became more convinced that I should linger with Ruby when I saw her sorrow still courting the creases around her eyes and mouth.

We could talk for a while, I thought, but I wanted to include Willy. I looked directly at him and offered my opinion of how he must feel, not being able to relay the answers that rang up in his mind like punched keys on a cash register. He again did not respond or act as if anything I thought was very important. He focused on Ruby and treated me like a customer. Willy was polite but disconnected from me.

"Ruby," I said, "would you tell me about how you happened to come to live in Gloucester?

"I guess you plan on staying here for a while if you are asking me a question like that," she said. Willy pushed back his chair; its legs scraped the hardwood floor. The three of us cringed. We had all become sensitive to the night, to every creak, every uninvited gust of wind against the windows. Buddy Baker had plucked an unseen primordial chord that left us afraid, fearful that he would return.

Willy Wu moved onto the bright, floral sofa in front of the television. He turned on a late night program.

"Willy, child, you got to take your medication," Ruby said. "Go on and get your backpack. I'll pour you a glass of water." She got up, winced as she straightened her knees, and walked slowly to the sink.

"What does Willy take medication for, Ruby?" I asked.

"Mostly to prevent him from having seizures," she said. "The boy is so finely wired that his electrical system can get overloaded and cause an epileptic episode."

Ruby returned to the table and added another tea bag to the pot. "His Mamma keeps a medical kit in his backpack for the times he sleeps over." Willy came back into the room and handed Ruby his bag. She reached inside and extracted a plastic container with seven compartments marked with the days of the week. Ruby helped him take the correct dosages: a tiny green triangle, two pink squares and one yellow round. When all the pills were ingested, Willy picked up the remote and began to flip channels.

My mind flashed to Nettles Cove, to Jack and the kids. There was a line-up of pharmaceuticals standing sentry for me in the kitchen. Annalise's cupcakes were thawed and waiting for pink icing. Jack had probably called the house two, maybe three times by now, the rings echoing in the stillness for only Yellow Dog to hear. All the kids must still be up watching television like Willy. I wrapped my arms across my chest to ward off a chill. The subtle fluctuations in my body's metabolism along with missed medication began to work against me. My body temperature seemed to be in a spiral. I pulled up the hood of my jacket.

Ruby walked back and forth a few more times between Willy and the kitchenette. Her movement sent her apron flopping hard against her broad middle, and the wisps of hair around her face swayed softly like a portable halo.

"You're all crunched up, child, like it's twenty below in here," Ruby said, stopping to stand in front of me, hands splayed on her hips. "Hold that cup in your hands, the tea is hot, it'll warm you some."

"Thanks, Ruby, I'm okay," I said. "Somewhere I read that you lose a lot of body heat out the top of your head. Have you ever heard of that?"

Ruby said no, and made one last trip over to Willy before she sat down on her rocker.

"My bald head is like a heat-loss speedway." I grinned at her.

"You got a good sense of humor, child, that's the best medicine for these times." She stretched her legs out in front of her and reclined her head against the upholstered portion of the rocker. "What do you suppose the good Lord was thinking when he took my Abe? I wonder about that sometimes, but I can't dwell on it for long." She patted her apron and smoothed her hair with an open palm. "I look at Willy, see how he is different, and ask the Lord why, but I never get a clear answer. Some days accepting life as it is, as it's supposed to be, isn't enough. I want more of a reason." She looked at me with wide eyes. "Something more concrete."

"You know what I want a damn good answer for?" I said, holding onto my cup and leaning across my elbow to Ruby. "Tell me why your good Lord makes people like Buddy Baker."

"Hudson," Ruby quieted the rocker with both feet set firm on the floor, "it is okay to have doubts. After I question my Lord, I tell him that Ruby Desmond is not perfect, and then I ask His forgiveness for my weak moments. As for the Baker boy, it isn't my good Lord's fault that Buddy's family did him wrong. Some folk got no business being parents, they got no business planting their seeds and letting them grow." Her face showed outrage at the thought.

"Hmm," I said. "Buddy scares me. Not just a goose bump kind of scared, but deeper, something more dreadful. He was a student of mine at the high school, always angling, throwing out his feelers to see just how far he could shove authority. The two of us locked horns almost every day. Buddy would get detention and very often end up having to face me for another hour or more. Days without confrontation were the days he was absent, and there were a lot of those."

I continued telling Ruby how I could feel his aggression seeping out by the way he looked at me. His eyes would narrow, leaving just a cat's iris visible, and his mouth would pull up on one corner into a smirk. I would speak to Buddy, and he would never look at me, never acknowledge that I held any power over him. We sparred mostly, exchanged barbs and traded insults.

The way he dressed set him apart from his peers. He wore his hair in a pompadour, slick on the sides and pulled down over his forehead. Buddy always wore a black tee under a loose fitting, long-sleeve shirt and straight-leg jeans that fell low on his leather, broad-toe boots. Another quirky thing was a large set of keys that hung from his belt. I counted them once and there were fifteen, ranging in size from a diary-opener to an old-fashioned metal gate turner.

His father never responded to the calls from the principal's office. It amazed me that Buddy even came to school because it was obvious that no one cared whether he could read, count or write. Yet the one thing that kept me from giving up on him completely was that he came on his own, and it appeared to be because he wanted to learn. He was adept at language and could switch from street talk to near perfect grammar in a blink. This did not make me less afraid of him. I knew in an intuitive way rather than by any tangible reason that I could explain, that he had a dark side, darker than most.

The school files did not contain the full details of Buddy's past, only that his mother was deceased, that he had at least four younger siblings and his father. There was information concerning a number of petty crimes, and notes about child abuse by his father and possibly other family members. Buddy's short stays with foster parents were noted, but after each one, he was inevitably sent home again. The time Buddy spent incarcerated as a juvenile delinquent was confirmed, but the reason was not given. An entry mentioned possession of a firearm but neglected to say whether the gun had been fired or not.

Anyone who read Buddy's file would probably be left wondering about the real truth. All of this, and none of this, made it clear to me that one day, some nothing-of-a-thing could set him off, and without warning, Buddy Baker would be dangerous.

Ruby kept rocking and listening with her full attention. My recollections of Buddy Baker barreled out from their hiding places and filled the tiny space around us. A particularly vivid memory of Buddy was of the day I saw him without his shirt on. It was the end of the school year and the temperature was unusually high for the shore. The girls were in skimpy shorts and revealing halters while the boys suffered through with souvenir tee shirts announcing past concerts and trips to the White Mountains. Buddy Baker had his jeans and boots on as usual, but above the waist his chest was bare. He was lean but muscular, as if he worked out daily. I had a sense that the closest Buddy ever got to the gym was push-ups on the pier and chin-ups off the bridge.

The first bell had rung and there was a rush of feet making their way down the halls and up the stairs from class to class. I came out of my room for no specific reason except to catch a breeze from all the activity passing by my door. Buddy's head appeared in the crowd; he emerged like Moses parting the sea. The students ahead of him turned their heads in a way reserved for those not wanting to be noticed, but still making an effort to see what is happening. His face held a look of mild annoyance, but otherwise he seemed oblivious to the whispers.

Buddy Baker had a dragon tattooed across his chest, his arms and his back, the kind of dragon that breathes fire and consumes sacrificial, pre-pubescent females. This was not a proud Chinese dragon infusing good fortune into his biceps. Instead, the greed and damaged ego of this scaled creature sent flames and angst into his muscles. Buddy's hair was naturally red, and the searing breath of the beast seemed to have singed each strand to the roots. The mouth of the dragon was wide open and shot flame down Buddy's left arm. The tail, arrow-like, stabbed out of his right. The body of the dragon sat on Buddy's back in a field of spikes and scales.

He strode by me and then turned, walked back, took both of my hands and pressed them onto his upper chest. The dragon undulated under my palms as Buddy flexed the toned muscles around his nipples. I was horrified. He released my wrists, allowing my arms to flap back to my sides, and walked away laughing.

TWELVE

"Do you think that boy will come back here tonight?" Ruby asked. She put her teacup down and stared at me for a long minute. The expression on her face had gone hard.

"I think he will. Buddy would never concede in any confrontation. He was not a white flag waver. Why don't you call the police, let them know Buddy's been here causing a disturbance. Tell them about the cigarettes and him calling you names," I said.

"The police won't come out on a night like this for that kind of nonsense. My Lord, a person can't see a hand in front of them with the snow coming down like it is. Calling would just be a waste of time."

"I wish you would reconsider, Ruby. Think about it. In the meantime, you should lock the door," I said.

"You're right, you're right," she repeated. "Willy," Ruby turned away from our conversation to get Willy's attention, "boy, go lock the front door please."

There was a note of urgency in her voice. Willy didn't move. He and the television had become one. Ruby grew impatient. "Now child, go lock that door right this minute." Her tone was tinged with fear of Buddy Baker's return.

Willy got up from his seat like a robot, his movements unbending. He jingled the keys in his pocket and walked stiff-limbed out into the store, across the aisles to the automatic door. He bypassed the buzzer and we heard the lock clunk as he turned the key. Ruby let out a sigh of relief and Willy Wu quickly resumed his place next to the remote control.

"I feel better now," Ruby said. She started rocking again, and a smile found its way to her lips. "Remember you asked me earlier to tell you about coming to Cape Ann? Well I was just thinking that Buddy Baker's grandaddy was a friend of my husband, Charlie Desmond. For good or for bad, those are the kinds of things that keep the world small."

"Can I ask what happened to Charlie?"

Ruby paused mid-rocking, the angle of her face picked up the glow from the television set. She held her answer on her tongue for a few moments, as if sorting through a list of responses. Once she had settled some information in her head she spoke with a clear voice.

"I got to start at the beginning, that way all the questions about my Charlie get answered."

"Do you mind talking about your past, Ruby?" I asked.

"No, child, I don't mind," she said. "Maybe God wants Hudson Catalina to be at Whales Market so Ruby Desmond can talk and clean out some stuff in her heart."

Perhaps this was true, but who knew? What we did know was that the snow ruled the night, cutting off neighbor from neighbor, family from family, and that the three of us were sitting in a warm room sharing tea.

"I was seventeen," she began. "Seventeen when my mamma put me on a bus headed north. I'd never been further than a few miles from home, but here I was leaving behind my mamma, brother and three little sisters. The Great Depression had hit the South hard. My daddy was fortunate to be one of a few dark-skinned men that had a steady job. He was a good man, generous and compassionate with what appeared to be a strong constitution. No one ever suspected that his heart was weak, and that it would give out on him in the middle of the day when the sun was high in the South Carolina sky. The loss of my daddy forced me to go out and look for work, and within weeks of his passing, a wealthy white man from Massachusetts hired me, Ruby Jackson, to nanny his children.

"His name was Jeremiah Bothwick, and he had known my daddy in the First World War. Mamma had sent Mr. Bothwick a copy of the obituary with a note explaining our circumstance. My mamma was never quite sure what passed between her husband and Mr. Bothwick, but she did know that the two had continued to communicate long after the war ended.

"The mountains of the Carolinas disappeared as I pressed my nose into the bus's dusty window. A wet film covered my face, some of it perspiration and some of it tears. The memory of my family became a blur against the highway's heat. My fellow passengers were crammed together all around me, like bales of cotton. Suitcases and belongings were overhead and on laps, each traveler moving away from what they knew towards the unknown. The journey took a few days and several bus stops. I kept to myself, afraid that talk would bring attention to my fears.

"Mr. Jeremiah Bothwick had a driver and car waiting when I arrived in the North Shore of Boston. His house was a grand affair set atop a hill overlooking the Atlantic Ocean. The Bothwicks were descendants of a Puritan family, one of the first to settle on Cape Ann in the mid–sixteen hundreds. Jeremiah owned a good chunk of the Harbor and various properties from Ipswich to Gloucester, including the one called Castle Mar.

"I'd never seen a shoreline or felt a salt breeze on my cheek, and I remember holding my bags, one in each hand, staring out at the sea and wondering if maybe someone had put a spell on my head. Many years later, when Jeremiah Bothwick was aged and near death, he made things right for his self. He told me about the bond between him and my daddy. But that was years after Jeremiah and me lived our own lives, to our own music, at our own pace.

"Comfortable with a life that made me responsible for others, I took easy to the care and cooking for the Bothwick household. There were three children. Tripp Bothwick, five years younger than me, was away at boarding school when I arrived. Mostly my job was to tend to Arabella and Emily Bothwick, ages six and three. I loved those little girls. They called me Mamma Ruby; still do, to this day.

"Jeremiah, he paid me a decent wage, and our agreement included an additional, undisclosed sum to be sent to my mamma once a month. This money was enough for her to buy a small house and school my three sisters and brother. It wasn't easy, but we managed to write now and then with news. Mamma and my sisters never came north, only my brother came once, and that was to tell me of mamma's passing. He said he didn't want to write such stuff in a letter so he came instead. I was close to birthing Abe at the time and wouldn't have been able to make a trip south. My brother stayed a few weeks with Charlie and me, taking in the sights and the ocean. We promised not to let distance keep us from being a family and we all kept that promise. These days, with only three of us left, we still get round to the telephone at holidays and birthdays. Two of my sisters passed some years back, more sad days for Ruby Desmond. But all of us, we thanked the Lord regular for the blessings he gave us, and I am quick to say that it wasn't just the Lord we had to thank, but our daddy, too."

Ruby stopped. "Am I boring you, child?" she asked. "All this talk about myself has got to be plain tiresome."

"No, Ruby," I answered. "Please tell me how you met your husband."

I looked over at Willy. His eyes seemed heavy. Only his right hand moved, dipping on occasion into the bowl of popcorn Ruby had set in front of him.

"Tripp Bothwick enlisted in the Navy after college." Ruby continued her story. "He and many other young men on Cape Ann had gone to fight World War II. There was only a handful of boys left behind that the military had declared unfit. Whatever disabled those few from war did not keep 'em from going to sea. A good fortune for the fishermen, because some of those young men that were overlooked made their livelihood out on the ocean. One of these was my Charlie, Charlie Desmond, six years behind me in age. He was the son of a Welsh fisherman. Their roots were set in Cardiff, Wales, and replanted here in Ipswich. Charlie cut his teeth at sea. Everything he learned came from his grandaddy and his papa. My Charlie's love of the ocean stayed with him till the day he passed. That man knew the ocean. He knew her moods like the sea was inside Charlie himself.

"I took to taking walks on my days off through the narrow streets of Gloucester to the Esplanade and Fishermen's Memorial. Psalm One Hundred Seven is engraved beneath the bronze statue. I was quite taken by the inscription and felt a kinship with that place. It was on one of these walks that I first met my Charlie.

"On this particular day, I arrived earlier than usual and found some of the fishermen still hauling in their catch. I stood off watching for a while and noticed a young man with hair the color of corn and skin ruddy from the salt and sun. He stood a head taller than the other men, his muscled frame deftly working the nets and crates. Unable to sit in my usual spot where I could dangle my feet in the water and spread open my lunch napkin, I settled down with my picnic on a makeshift bench. This set me out of the way of the fishermen but with a full view of the harbor.

"To be honest, I never paid much mind to fashion. My dresses were simple: cotton in the summer and wool in the winter. I didn't gussie up, I wore no makeup and braided my hair straight back off my face just like it is now. Primping for a boyfriend I never had and never set out to have was just plain silly. My life up to that day had not included romance. When I seen that tall young man I'd been watching come walking toward me, I wasn't sure what to do. Colored girls in the south ain't supposed to speak to white boys, and here I was thinking of what to say to that fair-haired boy heading my way. *You are not in South Carolina* is what kept going through my head as the young man stopped close enough for me to see one hazel-colored eye. In that instant I knew what kept that fine figure of a man from the battlefield. His right eye was milky white, with only a speck of the color that used to be there fading off in its middle. Uncle Sam was not about to sign up no Cyclops.

"That young man, he asked my name. I answered and asked him the same question. I offered him some biscuits from my basket. Charlie rested half of his body against a wooden post and talked fishing, all the while taking big bite after big bite of my biscuits. The fact that I was a colored woman didn't matter much to Charlie Desmond. He had a friendly nature and didn't follow no rules that required him to keep clear of dark-skinned girls.

"Our relationship stayed simple, just friendly talk. When we had chance meetings on the pier, both Charlie and me would eagerly share stories of our different lives. He didn't court me, not so you'd notice anyway. My Charlie never led me down the garden path making up this or that about the future.

"One Saturday morning, Jeremiah called me into his study. He asked me to sit and talk with him. I obeyed and wondered what was on his mind. Mr. Bothwick said that I was like family after eleven years of service. He said he didn't want me to think that he was treating me any different than his own kin. It seemed that some not-to-be-named person had been observing my friendship with

Charlie Desmond, and now Jeremiah wanted to know what Charlie's intentions were. I had no answer.

"The question put an end to my foolish thinking that here in the North the color of skin didn't matter none when it came to white boys. If Mr. Bothwick wanted me to end my conversations with Charlie Desmond, then I would. Jeremiah had said that perhaps this would be wise, and he thanked me once more for my excellent service to his household.

"What I didn't bargain on was Charlie's reaction to my decision. That man, he rose up to his full height, muscles tense under his shirt and fingers folded so tight against his palms that the fingernails done disappeared. There was no way that Charlie would stop seeing me, it wasn't nobody else's business, and then my Charlie stepped so close that his breath fell on my forehead and cheeks. He kissed me, the only man that would ever kiss me like that.

"Me and Charlie, we couldn't abide by Mr. Bothwick's wishes, so we kept on in secret. It was surely written down somewhere that our friendship, Charlie's and mine, should turn to love. When my time of the month came and went, we went out of state and found a Justice of the Peace who agreed to marry us. I became Mrs. Charlie Desmond and returned to Castle Mar, little Abe stirring inside my belly and my husband holding on to my hand.

"Jeremiah listened to our story and without any unkind words he told Charlie to clean out the old garden house near the back end of his property. This could be our home, Jeremiah said, if we wanted, and in exchange, I could stay on as a Bothwick employee. My Charlie was a reasonable man and knew the baby and I would have the best chance of a good life if we all stayed at Castle Mar. His job sent him away for long spells, and he wanted us to be safe, especially during our times of separation.

"This then was our beginning. People talked at first, but Charlie and me didn't let gossip get in the way of our love. Charlie was the best husband a woman could ever hope to have," Ruby said, pouring more tea. "These cups are part of a set that Jeremiah gifted us for our wedding, real English bone china."

"They're beautiful," I said. Ruby put her fingers on her temples and closed her eyes. She rocked a little then resumed her story.

"Abe was born in the fall of nineteen forty-five. He came while Charlie was out to sea. That baby boy was healthy, weighing in at almost ten pounds, but his birthing had been real hard on me and I was unable to bear more children. It was just the three of us after that, and since my duties to the Bothwick girls were less after Abe came, I could tend to my family without worry. These were the best years of our life.

"When my Charlie was not fishing, he was home being a good father to Abe and a loving husband to me. Once we were married, he had little to do with the sailors and regulars that frequented the local bars, but this didn't keep him from having many friends. Most people liked Charlie Desmond, and most forgave him for taking up with a colored girl. Among his assorted acquaintances was an ex-convict named Leg Iron Baker."

Ruby paused in her storytelling to squint at me, making a face that went with the memory.

"Leg Iron was one of the few who had an issue with our mixed marriage. The man was a bigot plain and simple. He had served time, that's how the nickname stuck, and incarceration only fueled his prejudice more. No one knew his given name, but in the chain of legacy, he was Buddy Baker's grandaddy. It's possible that Buddy's life was written well before he was even born," Ruby said, putting her hands together as if she were about to recite a prayer. "Buddy didn't come from the best stock, you know, that family is set in their ways and in their thinking. All they've done, child, is pass their narrow-mindedness down. Those folk are like sediment, they just settle at the bottom.

"Charlie once said that they should have called Leg Iron Baker *Women Hater Baker*, but that was when he'd had enough of Leg Iron. That was after my gentle Charlie, who couldn't hurt a fly, nearly killed Leg Iron with his bare hands. Buddy's grandaddy called me, Ruby Desmond, a white man's colored whore, and that set Charlie's jaw so tight that his jugular swelled purple along his neck. After that, Leg Iron pretty much kept his distance from Charlie. Except for those times when he'd had too much liquor and Leg Iron would set out to find Charlie to egg him on, but then he'd turn tail and run if Charlie came after him."

"What did Leg Iron do to go to prison?" I asked.

"Murder," Ruby answered. "The story was told a dozen different ways, but somehow he got off and came to live on Cape Ann. Killed his wife some said. Women got themselves into bad marriages and no one came running to help when fists flew. What went on in private, stayed private. If a woman sported a black eye, broken nose or arm, there was always a step to blame, or a wall. Buddy's grandma suffered the fate of so many abused wives of the times; their killers slept next to them, fathered their children and pulled the trigger. Whatever the true story, everyone knew that Leg Iron's victims were weaker than him, and," Ruby continued, "Charlie told me that Leg Iron Baker was not a man to turn your back on."

THIRTEEN

Ruby grew quiet for a few minutes.

"Charlie could judge a man's worth, and he knew Leg Iron Baker wasn't worth much. I think Charlie would tell us the same about Buddy, that the boy can't be trusted, and we should watch our backs." Ruby's voice was a whisper against the canned laughter from the television. She glanced over at Willy, his silhouette caught in the glow of the television screen. He was staring into the light, mesmerized by the faces of long dead actors, their voices decades silenced.

"What are you thinking, Ruby?" I asked.

"I'm thinking that even for Buddy Baker there was redemption. The good Lord provides for us all, and that boy is no exception. Buddy was given two people who touched his heart, *two people*, when some folk hardly get one."

"What two people?" I asked.

"His mamma," she said. "And Willy."

"Willy?"

"Yes, Willy. He was a friend to Buddy Baker."

I couldn't fathom it; Willy and Buddy?

"How could that be?" I said.

"Hudson," Ruby tapped her fingers on the table to make her point, "I know and you know just how godforsaken that Baker boy is, but Willy knows another side of him. Several years back, Buddy taught Willy how to row a boat. There was an old twelve-footer near the inlet one house down from the Wulinskys'. From what I've heard,

Willy would wander down to where the rowboat was tied up and sit in it for hours, slapping the air with a pair of imaginary oars.

"The story goes that one afternoon Buddy found Willy *rowing*, and instead of sending him off with a mean-fisted good riddance, Buddy took him out on the water with a pair of real oars. A short time later Willy, with the God-given knack of doing things over and over, was rowing. Lord, child, sweet Willy was rowing like a pro. He and Buddy went out on that wooden boat a couple, three times a week. The two formed an odd kinship that only Buddy and Willy understood."

"What happened to change that?" I asked.

"Life," Ruby said. "Some say the boat sank, others say that Buddy lost interest in Willy. I prefer to think it was the twelve-footer that gave out, but whichever is correct, one day Buddy stopped coming around, and soon after Willy started working at Whales Market."

"You said two people, Willy and Buddy's mother. I know she died but I don't know how or when."

"She passed when he was eight." Ruby glanced up as if heaven's gate was on her ceiling. "The boy hasn't been right since."

"What caused her death?" I said.

"Maybe you don't want to know the answer Hudson, maybe we talked enough about Buddy Baker tonight," Ruby answered.

"Just tell me how she died, Ruby." My need to know surpassed my fear of finding out and turned my throat dry. This triggered a tickling cough. Ruby went to the sink and filled a glass with tap water. She came back, handed it to me and resumed rocking. My question had soaked into the crevices at the corner of her mouth. Her lips were drawn flat against her teeth as if locking out her response.

"I'd rather talk about my Charlie than to waste time telling things that won't make a difference in knowing." Ruby slid forward in her seat, her face close to mine. "Remember, child, there is a purpose to everything. People come and go in our lives, just like my Charlie, just like your ma and Buddy's mamma."

"Okay," I said with obedience, "but tell me more about your husband."

"Not much to tell until nineteen fifty-nine." Ruby looked down at her hands. "That was the year Charlie passed."

She clucked her tongue as she had earlier in the evening. It seemed to signal something deep inside.

"Charlie went out to sea less often than he did when he was younger. He was thirty-seven years old in fifty-nine. The sea was still in his veins. He was at his best when surrounded by water, but the years mellowed him, and Charlie happily split his time between land and sea to be with our family. Jeremiah gradually took my Charlie on as a handyman for Castle Mar. He was clever and could fix just about anything.

"It was early June and Castle Mar was preparing for the wedding of Emily Bothwick. Tents were being set up on the sprawling lawn behind the main house, along with tables and chairs for the ceremony and reception afterwards. Everyone had a list of chores to carry out, and Mr. Bothwick had me in charge of the whole event. I barked orders at my inexperienced help and sent Abe and Charlie on continuous errands. The kitchen was bustling with china and glassware, all being properly cleaned and polished for Saturday's celebration. It was Wednesday, the third, I'll never forget that day, and Charlie had just got back from his fourth round trip to town. He had Castle Mar's pick-up truck stacked with round tables, and he and Abe were unloading them.

"I was all business, not in a mind for clowning or jokes, and had been losing my patience with his and Abe's silly antics. The two of them began rolling the tables instead of carrying them, discovering this to be good fun. Their laughter spilled out from the backyard, and once more I stuck my head out from the kitchen to tell them to quit fooling around. Abe, who was a child quick to obey, he looked at his daddy with a maybe-we-better-stop look.

"He told me later that Charlie had winked at him and tiptoed up the porch steps. Charlie waited for me to come out again and grabbed my shoulders, turning me to face him. Then my husband kissed me, a long kiss, dipping my head down to one side like a happy ending in a movie. When I came out of Charlie's embrace, I pretended to be annoyed. The truth is that even today I can still remember how strong his embrace was and the feel of my skirt as I smoothed the creases made from being crushed against him.

"I clucked at Charlie, but he knew me, he could see the softness in my lips. When I turned away and opened the screen door, I heard something heavy fall to the ground. At first I thought something got knocked over, but as I came round, there was Charlie, all six feet four of him, crumpled onto the ground like he was made of paper.

"The coroner's report said that Charles Desmond died from a massive heart attack. My husband, the only man besides my Daddy that I loved, had succumbed to the exact same fate. Jeremiah wanted to postpone the wedding, but Abe and I wouldn't hear of it. Charlie didn't like a fuss and he would not have wanted the occasion to be marred by his passing. The wedding went on without incident, and Charlie was cremated and buried at sea a few weeks later. His shipmates on the *Harbor Queen* swabbed her decks and shined her brass fittings. They dropped anchor several miles off shore and with me, Abe and Jeremiah Bothwick as passengers, Charlie Desmond was laid to rest on Mother Ocean's floor.

"I'm a woman of great faith," Ruby said. "When Charlie passed, I relied on my belief in God to help me through those long days and even longer nights."

"Weren't you angry?" I asked her. "His dying just like your Daddy is like my mother and I dying of breast cancer."

"First off, child, you are not dead yet; and second, things don't go according to our plan, no way, no how." Ruby made her point by thrusting her head back into her rocker and pushing off hard on the runners. "I'm not unfeeling to your situation, child, but the truth is you have already decided what is going to happen and that's plain crazy. God isn't to blame for these unfortunate times in our lives."

"Who is then?" I asked.

"Just like I said before, I never get the answers I want when I ask." She made a circle with her finger in the air. "If you're asking me, *which you are*, I'll tell you that life's a circle and we go around like the spokes on a wheel. Sometimes we're happy, our faces in the light, and sometimes the wheel thrusts us into harsh places of darkness and despair. But we have to believe that it keeps going round, back into the light. Never give up hope."

Ruby settled her hands on her lap, stroking the bulge in her apron as she continued.

"My son convinced me to get my high school diploma. He thought it would fill the emptiness and offer me a challenge. I attended classes and finished in Abe's senior year of high school just a few months after Abe had been accepted at a Massachusetts teachers' college. It was such a relief to be done with my studies, and I had no college aspirations, but Abe and Jeremiah Bothwick felt differently.

"Jeremiah came to me with a business proposal. He was considering purchasing a small market with an attached house on a parcel of land north of the harbor. It would take some time to work out the details and even more time to do the renovations necessary for the future Whales Market to open. He wanted me, Ruby Desmond, to manage the store for him while I attended college and, once I graduated, the store, the house and the property would be signed over to Abe and me.

"Lord, child, I just couldn't believe our good fortune. The prospect of being independent, of moving from Castle Mar to our own house near the harbor; I was no fool child, I agreed.

"The next four years were spent turning Whales from a one-aisle beer and cigarette variety store into a five-aisle mini-mart. Mr. Bothwick was true to his word and the day of my college graduation he handed over the deed to Whales.

"Do you see what I mean, child?" she asked me. "None of this would have happened had my Charlie not passed. I'm doing what I'm supposed to be doing, and that's the thread of hope that helps to mend my broken parts."

I didn't know what to say to Ruby. She made a good argument for believing in a higher power. There was no immediate urge to return to the fold, but I was softening. Some of my angst had dissipated, and tiny bits of me could see how foolhardy and selfish I'd been.

Ruby started to speak; her voice lifted my thoughts and set them aside. She told me that soon after Abe's college graduation, it became apparent that, unless he had a high lottery number, he was going to get called up for the draft.

"Despite this very real threat to our peaceful life, Abe accepted a job teaching in Roxbury, where he was to start after Labor Day. Mid-May through early July he worked with me at Whales. He helped me move what furniture we owned from Castle Mar to the house above the market. Those eight weeks were a gift from the Almighty. Not since Abe was a small child had I had the opportunity to spend so much time with my son.

"Then the Selective Service notice came saying that Abraham Lincoln Desmond needed to report to Fort Dix. This would be his induction into the army. Me and Abe talked that night, a long, soul-searching talk that ended at the light of morning. Late in July, he joined the Marines. My son went in as a Second Lieutenant and that suited him. The experience would make him wiser, he told me, and I shouldn't worry because he'd be back in one year.

"The rest of Abe's story is part of history," Ruby said. "When the officers came to tell me that Abe was missing in action, I collapsed right out front there, between aisles three and four."

I turned my head involuntarily to peek out of the doorway at the spot where Ruby had fainted.

Ruby must have seen the turbulence of her life reflected in my eyes because she reached over to touch my hand. "I'm going to tell you one last story," she said. "This is about my Daddy and Jeremiah. Then you've got to pack up your things and get on home."

"Okay," I said.

"Jeremiah Bothwick outlived his wife and son," Ruby said. "Mrs. Bothwick passed away the summer before my arrival. There had been other nannies in those first months after her death, but none that the family sought to keep permanent. I felt blessed that the children took to me and I to them. As for Jeremiah, he wore the cloak of the widower like a mantle of monogamy. He never re-married or showed interest in any suitable, available female, choosing instead to live out the rest of his life devoted to his family and deceased wife. This was something I admired in him, and something that I was proud of in myself, always feeling married to my Charlie and dedicated to our son.

"Jeremiah was in his nineties when Tripp passed away and the dear man wasn't ever right after that. He willed himself to pass, at first becoming forgetful and eventually needing twenty-four-hour home care. I took on as many shifts as I could, working at Whales then going up to Castle Mar. He relied on me to be close by, and in the early stages of his condition, Jeremiah talked the hours away, filling the time telling stories of his past.

"'Please tell me about you and my Daddy in the Great War,' I had asked him. The ravages of sorrow and old age had left his face with two great hollows for cheeks. When I asked my question, the one I'd longed to have answered since childhood, Jeremiah wept.

"My father was one of about a hundred thousand colored soldiers to be sent to Europe when President Wilson declared War in April nineteen seventeen. He left a young wife and me, barely one year old. Jeremiah was among the hundreds of thousands of white soldiers sent to France for the same reason. It should have been unlikely that the two men, so different in color and background, would cross paths. White officers seldom had occasion to have an exchange with colored soldiers relegated to Services of Supply. The United States, at that time, did not give colored soldiers adequate training or the equipment necessary to perform their military duties. These men became laborers and stevedores, passed-over but brave individuals relegated to mess tents and loading docks. Late in nineteen seventeen, Jeremiah was awaiting orders, biding his time at a French army post. It was here that he first encountered my daddy, Abraham Lincoln Jackson.

"Abraham was bareheaded, hauling supplies to camp in the pouring rain.

" 'Good evening, Major, sir,' he said to Jeremiah. His coat was soaked clear through to his skin, every part of him shining wet against the downpour. Jeremiah was walking with two fellow officers and came up short when the soft-spoken Abraham stepped aside. The others made racist insults and continued walking.

"'Looks like you could use some dry clothes, young man,' Jeremiah answered back. Abraham tossed the huge sack over one shoulder and looked directly at him.

"'I do appreciate your respect and concern, Major,' he said. 'I'll get myself dry later.' He saluted and continued his work.

"Jeremiah seemed relieved that he could tell me this story, the worn edges of its waiting at last spread out. He and my daddy were to see each other a few more times over the next several weeks. Something drew them together, Jeremiah told me, something unexplained.

"The French were training colored troops, and Abraham was chosen to join them. Once that happened, Jeremiah doubted he would ever see Abraham Lincoln Jackson again.

"The United States' decision to join her allies in the Great War was the turning point for victory. Six months later, in one of the final battles of the war, Jeremiah and his men were scattered within the French countryside. Casualties were high and supplies low.

"Their orders were to continue to push back the enemy, but after long hours of walking in regimented columns, the infantry were tired. Jeremiah ordered them to dig in and rest for a few hours. His decision came about the same time an enemy squadron took off for their location. They launched a surprise attack while his men slept. Bombs rained over them, blowing soldier after soldier out of their bunkers. Jeremiah was badly hit. His left leg appeared to be blown apart, and there was blood spouting out of a hole in his right thigh.

"Hundreds of infantrymen moved along the trodden field, dodging enemy fire coming out of the sky. Major Bothwick lay on his back, arms out crucifix style. Men ran by him, holding guns tight against their chests, eyes straining to see the unseen. There was some pain by then, a deep-seated throbbing that told Jeremiah the hemorrhaging was fatal. Death came and sat beside him, in no particular hurry, or so it seemed, to take his soul. He closed his eyes and prayed to the Lord, not the Our Father or a memorized standard, but a prayer of his own invention.

"The ground shook from the pounding of boots and the voices of the troops droned like worker bees. A breeze stirred in his ear; a gentle whisper spoke his name.

"'Major Bothwick, sir, is you alive?'

"Jeremiah opened his eyes to see not the Angel of Death, but Abraham Lincoln Jackson.

"'My legs are torn up,' Jeremiah said. My father tied a tourniquet to stem the bleeding and with the same agility that he used tossing sacks of potatoes and flour, he hoisted Jeremiah over his shoulder and began to run. He sprinted and then ran for miles, never resting until he found the field hospital. Military personnel immediately tried to separate them, Daddy being ordered to go with his own kind. Jeremiah, too weak to protest, managed to put a hand out to stop him from leaving and motioned Daddy to come close.

"'Thank you,' he said, 'you saved my life. You are a hero. I will never forget what you did today.'

"'We are friends, Major,' Daddy said so that only Jeremiah could hear. 'That's what friends do for each other. Let's keep this between friends, sir. It will be best for both of us if you tell no one what happened in that field.'

"Jeremiah nodded, and Abraham Lincoln Jackson was gone.

"When the war ended, Jeremiah Bothwick found Abraham Lincoln Jackson's address. He wrote to him extending his gratitude and his desire to compensate Abraham for his heroism. My Daddy would have none of it. His letter to Jeremiah reassured Mr. Bothwick that what happened on that day in the Great War was an act of friendship, and no monetary payment was necessary. Their writing continued until the day Jeremiah received the letter from my Mamma. He then made it his responsibility to take care of all of us, Abraham's family, and in order not to insult the pride of his dead friend, Jeremiah began by bringing me, Ruby Jackson, to Castle Mar."

Willy had come back to the table sometime during the telling of Jeremiah's story. Ruby patted him on the head. He yawned and smiled a sleepy smile back at her.

"You do like that story, don't you, boy?" she said. Willy's smile broadened showing small square teeth. "He's heard it a dozen times." She looked at me. "But Willy here never tires of it."

"Hero," Willy said and kept smiling at Ruby. Small kernels of popcorn clung to his chin and one corner of his mouth. Ruby used her napkin to wipe them off.

"Yes," she said, "my Daddy was a hero. But now, all my stories are told and we need to get ourselves some sleep. I need you to turn off the television, Willy. Your mamma will have my hide for letting you stay up so late." Willy made a guttural noise in answer to Ruby. He got up and clicked off the set.

I looked at the clock and saw that it was close to midnight. It was time to go home. My jacket clattered as I got up from the table. Ruby and I laughed.

"Go on and finish up, child. Get yourself down aisle three, and then you get on home. Leave the dishes, I got nothing but time tonight."

"Thanks, Ruby," I said stepping by her. She reached around and hugged me. My arms were straight at my sides and her embrace enveloped me like I was a bundle of twigs. I felt myself sag and lean into the broad arms of Ruby Desmond.

"You've given me a renewed sense of life, Ruby. Just being here tonight, hearing your stories, learning more about Willy, has showed me how foolish I was to give up hope. I thought I had no choices left. I thought all along that cancer would be by executioner." My lips brushed the white starched collar of her blouse. "I'm rethinking my party plan for Annalise's birthday. Maybe it would be better to concentrate on her turning five and not worry about what will come later. You're right, Ruby. We don't know what is going to happen next or how we are going to die."

"I'm glad you feel that way, Hudson, because I've given you nothing that you haven't already given," she said still holding me in her arms. "That's the way the Lord makes it work."

"Go on," she spun me towards the store, "go on, finish up and get home safe."

"Okay," I said and headed once again down aisle three.

Ruby sent Willy to the back of the store to go to the bathroom; she was concerned that he would have an *accident* after drinking so much tea.

"He can have times that are embarrassing." She pulled me aside to share this information in a whisper. "His Mamma always sends a change of clothes, just in case," she added. "We don't want to make too much of it," she said. "That boy is such a dear, do you know he won't go upstairs to bed unless I'm going up. He doesn't like to leave me alone down here."

I smiled at her, thinking how the two of them took care of each other in their own ways.

It didn't take me long to put back handfuls of party supplies. My final choices, the ones for a girl's fifth birthday, were in my hands when a loud pounding startled me. The windows shook and I dropped everything. Instinct drove my hands to my head. My mind raced, thinking that the roof was about to cave in. The pummeling grew louder, but it wasn't above us, no, the racket came from the front of the store. Ruby ran past aisle three. I didn't think she could move that fast. I started back up the aisle to see what was happening then stopped and turned as Ruby came up the opposite end. Her face was red and her mouth open, gasping.

"Buddy..." she managed to say as she moved around the fallen party goods trying not to lose her footing. The lights flickered—on and off, on and off in chilling sync with the two-fisted hammering against the frigid glass.

FOURTEEN

"What you want?" Ruby said. "White trash," she muttered coming back into my aisle again. She was soaked with perspiration and still having difficulty breathing. "That Baker boy is shaking money through the window for his almighty beer. I've a mind to just let him stand out there and freeze to death."

I'd gone back to pick up my fallen party items. My hands were shaking and I slid my fingers under my armpits. *Don't let him in.* The words failed me so I shook my head at Ruby with as much strength as I could, and tried again to speak.

"Don't let him in, Ruby." This time the sentence had sound. "He's going to start trouble. Remember what we talked about."

She interrupted me.

"No, no ... he'll just keep banging until he cracks all my windows."

"Don't let him in," I repeated. "You said he couldn't be trusted."

But Ruby didn't listen.

"That glass is going to cost me a fortune of money," she muttered, passing me and heading towards the back of the store. "Willy," she called out, "you got the keys, child?"

I don't know where Willy had been hiding, but when Ruby called for him he just appeared. He took quick, short steps from his unseen place of safety and held the keys up for Ruby to see.

"Let him in," she said to Willy. "I'll tend the cash register."

"No, Ruby," I said, fear forming on the roof of my mouth like a thick paste. She brushed by me without answering. "You can't let him in, Ruby." My tongue grappled with the fright layered on my palate.

She disappeared from my sight and Willy headed for the front door. There was a clatter of keys and, without seeing, I heard Willy drop the keys once, then twice. All the while Buddy Baker kept slamming his fists against the window. Once the door opened, the buzzer sounded like it was just another day, just another customer, just another sale.

Buddy came in like a dervish, pumped up and roaring.

"Willy, hey man, I didn't see you before, what's up?" he said. Willy didn't answer, or at least I couldn't hear his answer from aisle three. Buddy headed straight down the first aisle to the beer.

"Hey *you*," he yelled over the aisles to Ruby, "get me a carton of cigarettes. I got some fucking money and I don't want to hear any of your mother-fucking lip about me and my beer and smokes." He paused. "Willy dude, you're my friend, and it pains me that you work for such a bitch."

I made myself shrink against the canned frostings and powdered sugar. Buddy was making these hateful remarks out of my sight, not yet into Ruby's face where I guessed his saliva would come out with his words like venom from a snake or fire from a dragon. There was nowhere for me to hide, and I wanted to hide. Worse than that, I wanted to call Jack, but I hadn't brought my phone—never remembered to bring my phone—and this was one time I wished I had. Jack said having the phone was good for emergencies. As I clung to the food coloring and plastic tubes of ready-made icing, I knew that this was an emergency. I started to cry. The tears came in silent streams, crisscrossing my nose and encircling my lips. Having cancer scared me, but having Buddy Baker cursing at Ruby across five aisles of Whales Market put a fear in me that I'd never felt before.

Buddy was still in aisle one. He told Willy to go up front and get him a grocery cart. Willy lumbered past my aisle, eyes straight ahead, arms and hands jutted out like wings. The clamor he made detaching one grocery cart from the others filled the momentary quiet of the store. Willy grunted each time he yanked but the carts stayed stuck, and he struggled harder. Ruby intervened, telling Willy he wasn't a slave to that no-good white trash. Soon Willy Wu pushed past aisle three with the freed wagon. The distinct swish sound of a pop-top opening came from aisle one. I imagined Buddy downing a beer and looking at the girlie magazines arranged discreetly along the wall, out of reach of young hands.

As Willy neared aisle one, Buddy's cell phone rang. The ring tone was monophonic, a short, one-note-at-a-time rendering of a Spanish masterpiece. How strange, I thought, not being able to associate Buddy with symphonic music.

"Hey, Dude," Buddy answered. He listened to his caller for a few seconds then told whoever was on the other end that he was loading up on beer and cigarettes at Whales. The caller maybe wasn't that impressed with Buddy's shopping list because Buddy's voice grew angry. "You're just giving me shit," he said. "Diane gave me shit tonight, man, and she's fucking sorry she did."

There was no more elaboration about Diane, but the call soon ended with Buddy telling his caller that he was fucking tired of listening to his crap.

Willy must have gotten the cart down the aisle because now I could hear Buddy dropping six-packs. The bottles clanged and he cursed. The call had obviously bothered him, the caller having the power to turn Buddy inside out.

"That prick is no friend of mine, Willy. Do you know what he said? Fuck, Willy, that dude said I owed him money and I should bring him beer and butts. Son of a bitch says I cheated him at cards and I fucking better pay up." As he spoke Buddy slammed pack after pack of bottles into the wagon.

I slid silent onto the floor. My knees were giving out, and I had to pull myself together. If Buddy saw me I knew it would tick him off. I hoped Ruby would avoid drawing attention to my presence in aisle three.

"Willy, drink a fucking beer, man," Buddy said. "The only thing that's going to make you and me feel better is a nice cold beer. Willy was silent, probably answering Buddy with a shake of his head.

"Fuck, dude, don't you start pissing me off too."

"What are you doing over there, Buddy Baker? Leave Willy be. He don't need no beer or no cussing from your mouth. He's a good boy, not like the likes of you."

Ruby's voice was cross. I wished she wouldn't speak with that tone. It was just going to infuriate him more, she needed to nod and smile, say yes sir, no sir, pacify him, get rid of him. I clenched my teeth as I heard the wagon moving up aisle one. If I tried to concentrate on getting my balance, if I was successful, I thought maybe I could sneak back into the rest room. But my legs were rubber and only my thoughts had mobility.

Buddy hadn't answered Ruby; they were at a brief stand-off, one waiting for the other to have the last word. His footsteps grew louder as he made his way closer to aisle three.

"Mother-fucking black bitch," he found his voice, "you got my smokes?" He walked past aisle three. Willy pushed the cart and Buddy swigged a beer. Neither of them looked my way. I drew in my breath, trying to quiet my quickened heart. Anxiety was an unwelcome visitor in my circulatory system, sending panic-stricken messages to my brain that produced a hard pressing pain mid-chest.

"You got no call to talk to me like that," Ruby said. "You're just pure white trash, boy, and you don't scare me none." Two six packs were slammed onto the counter. I made a fist and put it in my mouth.

"Why you got to do that, boy?" Ruby wasn't letting up.

"You're pissing me off, old woman," Buddy said. "Shut the fuck up!" The bottles smacked once again and I heard what sounded like a scuffle. "You hear me?" Buddy's voice hissed. There was no answer, no response from Ruby, until a cough broke the silence, a sputtering and gasping filled the night. I strained to catch a glimpse of them reflected in the window and bit down hard on my fist. Buddy had Ruby on her knees, her blouse caught up in his free hand twisted dangerously close to her neck.

"Don't fuck with me tonight," he said, putting his face into hers. Ruby pulled her head back and spit at him. He would surely kill her.

Willy Wu appeared in the reflection. He went down on his knees next to Ruby and put his arms around her.

"What are you doing, dude?" Billy let go of Ruby and went back to the grocery cart. "I'm not *really* going to kill her, Willy. I was just making a point, man. If you care about that black bitch so much, then okay, I won't mess with her." Buddy kept muttering and swearing as he slammed his beer onto the counter.

Willy helped Ruby up and she moved over to the checkout, keeping silent. The old-fashioned cash register tallied each item with a distinct cha-ching.

"Paper or plastic?" Willy said, now back at the end of the counter ready to bag Buddy's purchase. The question from Willy came out clear and audible, the first words I'd heard him say since Buddy's return. "Paper or plastic" were words familiar to Willy, part of his job and part of his routine. As Ruby checked Buddy out, it didn't matter to Willy that Buddy had bullied his way back into Whales. Once reinstated to his duties, Willy became who he was everyday; Ruby's grocery cart collector and bagger.

"I don't fucking care, dude. Just fucking put the beer back in the wagon. Okay, dude?"

Even in the glass reflection it was apparent that Buddy was having difficulty focusing. Perhaps it was the sound of Willy's voice, or maybe he just needed another beer. He paced back and forth as Ruby rang up the order. He seemed suddenly at a loss as to what to do next. One hand slipped inside his jacket and pulled out a cigarette, Buddy flicked a lighter and the tip seared back as he inhaled.

"Do you smoke, dude?" Buddy asked Willy. This time I could see Willy shake his head. "Dammit, Willy, you need to get some vices. Working here is making your ass too fucking holy."

Willy placed two cigarette cartons in a plastic bag and laid them on top of the beer. His silence seemed to unnerve Buddy even more. Ruby waited for Buddy to pay. He drank a few more gulps of beer and finished his cigarette, grinding it out on the floor. Ruby kept still. Buddy pulled out his wallet from his jacket pocket. He laid out some bills on the counter and Ruby opened the cash register drawer. She made change and laid it down on the counter. Willy rearranged the plastic bag several times, finally putting it under his arm. He took hold of the cart's handle with both hands and pushed it towards the exit. One more pass by aisle three, I held myself tight. The two went toward the door. No head turned, no eyes looked into the periphery. I was safe.

The buzzer went off and the door opened. I let out a long breath and stood up. The door was still open. I could feel the cold and wind invading the warm market. Buddy must have gone to get his truck. I couldn't see any reflections, but I heard the over-sized engine and felt the vibration when a door slammed. At the opposite end of the store, Ruby took a few steps and stopped near aisle five, her hands on her hips, waiting. Buddy's voice rose and fell barking orders to Willy who handed him the beer from just inside the door.

"Close the door, child," she said. "You'll catch your death."

I couldn't see Willy, but I didn't hear the door make that comforting whoosh that closing it creates. Ruby took a few more steps. "Willy," she said his name in a pleading tone as if her whole intention could be carried in one word.

Willy stood on the threshold, the door to Whales wide open. Ruby came to the top of aisle three, she looked at me and back at Willy, her face determined. Don't speak to me, I prayed, not before Buddy is in his truck and the door to Whales is closed.

"That boy just boils my old woman's blood. He makes me so angry that I'll have to pray to the good Lord for forgiveness later. Something has gone and made him agitated and I don't think it's the storm or his forgotten money either. I told you he was no good through and through, and maybe you *should* know what happened to his mamma. Maybe knowing will allow us to feel some empathy towards Buddy Baker even if it appears that he's run out of redemption."

She kept her eyes fastened to the door as she asked her question. "Do you still want to know?"

Nothing was going to break my silence, not even my former need to know about Buddy's mamma, and anyway, Ruby didn't expect an answer. She was talking to me but only in the sense that I could hear, not for me to speak.

"I've heard his mamma was a beauty, a good god-fearing woman. It's a mystery why she would take up with the likes of Buddy's daddy. Young love is more passion than logic, and somewhere between the two she said I *do* to a sinful man. They lived in New Hampshire near her family. Buddy was the oldest of four children and the only boy. His mamma favored him and he adored her, adored her so much he killed her." Ruby's eyes flicked towards me then back to her vigil.

I was still busy being small and was unprepared for Ruby's revelation. It caught me so off guard that the shelf behind my head rattled its contents as I leaned into it, and all the time I thought she had died of cancer; selfish me.

"Killed her," Ruby repeated. "That boy heard his daddy beat his mamma night after night until one evening Buddy took a twenty-two out of the gun closet, put in a clip, and went after his father. Misfortune awaited. Buddy hid behind the bedroom curtains and watched while his daddy took his mother against her will. An eight-year-old boy has no business seeing such abuse. When Buddy's father was finished, he moved off Buddy's mamma. It was then that Buddy raised the gun to fire and as he did, his mamma sat up in bed. The shot hit her square in the chest."

Why is she telling me this now, I thought? Why, when she should be silent and passive until Buddy "killed-his-own-mother" Baker is gone? The draft created by the open door made me shiver. I walked closer to Ruby, keeping one hand on the candy shelf to steady me. The thought of Buddy's mother shattered into fragments by her little boy sent the hair on my arms straight up.

"The boy has no conscience anymore," Ruby said. "The worst has already happened to him and nothing else matters."

One cluck, two clucks of her tongue, Ruby's impatience grew. She tapped her right foot and drummed ten fingers on her hips. I could hear Buddy shouting at Willy, the blizzard's flow picking up his annoyance, something about only having two hands, and then Ruby was moving her lips, talking to me again.

"So he killed his dear mamma and he nearly killed me. That boy had my neck and I could feel myself going." She used her hands as animation for her rapid speech. "If it wasn't for Willy …"

She narrowed her eyes at me as if regarding me for the first time. I had gotten close enough to almost touch her. I pressed my finger against my lips, a silent plea for her to be quiet. When she kept on, I raised my hand and made a knife like gesture across my throat. She cocked her head like a child who was bewildered and confused.

"Why are you clowning at me, Hudson? I got no time for games."

She shook her head and stepped right in front of me. I let go of the shelf and attempted the slice-across-my-neck motion again, but as I did this, my fingers connected with a display of miniature candy hearts. One after the other, the plastic containers toppled onto each other like dominos, until they ran out of shelf and hit the floor. Ruby's face turned slowly away from mine. She looked over her shoulder.

The hum of Buddy's truck engine had gone silent.

Buddy stood at the top of aisle three, listening and watching.

FIFTEEN

My hand stopped mid-air and my eyes went wide. I was a pillar of salt, a paralyzed fly. He stared at me for a few seconds, snow caught up in his cap and melting down his jacket. Buddy's hands were bare and bright red from the cold; he held them to his mouth and blew into the tunnel made by his fingers. No one spoke. Those few seconds were like our future; unsure.

"Well, I'll be fucking damned," Buddy said. He pushed back his cap and sprigs of red hair escaped like hot lava. "Hey, how come you're not dead?" He pointed an icy finger at me. "You look like a fucking cue ball, Teach. God's payback, right?"

I dropped my arm and stayed silent. Ruby turned to face him.

"You got your beer, boy, just leave and let us have some peace." Her voice was tinged with scorn, but it didn't matter to Buddy. His eyes bounced and flashed.

"Old woman, you were hiding Teach on me and that doesn't make me happy. You've pissed me off for the second time in one night and I am definitely not pleased."

He strode up to Ruby and shoved her into the shortening and oil shelf so hard that it collapsed. Ruby's arms went behind her. She reached for something stable and found nothing. She went backward and backward until she went down too. He looked down at her and laughed.

"Teach and me, we got some history, right, Teach?" Buddy took a can of lard in his right hand and flung it down aisle three. It smashed into a display of Kleenex sending small tissue packets scattering onto the floor. He unbuttoned his jacket and took out a cigarette. He drew his fingers along the shaft, and put it between his lips. The lighter sparked and a single arc of flame shot out, enveloping the waiting end.

Ruby got onto her knees.

"What's got into you boy? You are just like your grandaddy. That Baker apple doesn't fall far from the tree."

I put my hands out to help her up. Buddy turned his back on us. He kicked away some of the fallen groceries and went back to the top of the aisle.

Willy Wu appeared. His face was crimson from the storm, and his large hands, in cut-off wool gloves, tugged at his trousers. He looked sheepishly at Ruby and me.

"Do you need to use the restroom, Willy?" Ruby said.

He shifted from foot to foot, nodded yes, and started to head for the bathroom.

"Where you going, dude?" Buddy said. "Nobody goes anywhere unless I tell them they can, do you hear me?" Willy looked at Ruby and back at Buddy.

"The child just needs to use the toilet," Ruby said. "Why you talking like that? So now you're going to pick on poor Willy?"

Buddy flicked his cigarette at Ruby.

"Listen, bitch, I don't want any of your mouth. Willy stays here until I say different. Besides I want to hear from the teacher. What have you got to say, Teach?" He lit another cigarette, took a drag, held it, then sent the smoke back out through his nose and mouth.

My mind's eye saw Buddy in detention, seated in the last row of my classroom. One arm was slung behind his chair, the other twirled a pencil in two fingers—the same two fingers that pulled the trigger that killed his mamma and sent him to a home for juvenile delinquents. Ruby's exposure of Buddy's past *did* make a difference in knowing. I saw what had eluded me as his teacher, all the cruelty in Buddy's life. His mother's death overshadowed Buddy's very being. He had been chosen, by an unseen force, to lose his mother too.

I knew now what drew us together, knew the adhesive that connected me to him. I tried to grab the raft of *knowing* as it floated by, tried to pull myself up onto the slippery rubber sides and get in next to Buddy and defuse him. But it was no use. The undercurrent of anger was too strong.

No matter what I said to him, now or in my classroom, for good or for bad, Buddy Baker was just a punk, full of ridicule and disrespect. I would ask him, back then, how long Buddy, how long can we keep this up, you and I, teacher and student, in this standoff of contempt? In answer, he would look me up and down, a slow grin sewn to his face.

Sometimes when I got home from work I'd take my frustration out on the cabinets, drawers, anything that could be slammed. I'd bang until the racket drove Jack out of his office and down to the kitchen to listen to my babble.

"I don't get it," I'd say to Jack. "Why am I so vulnerable to Buddy's insults?" Jack would let me spew for a while, burn off steam until I went limp and finally sat down. He would tell me that I was not going to change Buddy Baker, that what Buddy was went deep into the folds and layers of his being. Sixteen years of dealing with verbal and physical abuse had created a nasty junkyard dog. This kind of animal lacks attention and affection. Buddy was raised to be mean. If all of this could be removed, then maybe, as a teacher, I might have a chance, but it was unlikely and the reality was clear: I had become his whipping post.

"Buddy is a loner," Jack tried to explain to me. "He's never going to be accepted by his peers because he can't replant his family tree.

For one thing, the men he emulates hate women. They get wives and girlfriends pregnant and then beat them for giving birth to another mouth to feed. It's a vicious circle, like a dog chasing its tail."

I stood with my back pressed to assorted flavors of puddings and Jell-O, confronted by a Buddy who was now in his twenties with the very same chip on his shoulder and the very same tail. He looked directly at me, uncaring of Willy Wu and Ruby Desmond. My reflection was in his eyes, and it was the woman I had confronted almost one day ago. The one I threw my shoe at, the one who wanted to die, skin and bones, all teeth and no hair. That was who he saw. Had I learned anything from my conversations with Jack or more recently with Ruby? Did I grasp any clearer how to reach that one thread that hung off Buddy Baker, the one with the power to reel him in? I didn't think so. How was I to answer a predator like Buddy?

"Fuck, Teach, did they cut your tongue off with your boobs?" Buddy taunted me. Ruby clucked, her jaw muscle twitched and tightened from ear to chin with every wasted minute I stayed silent.

"It's my daughter's fifth birthday." My sentence came out with a stutter. "I'm buying decorations for her cupcakes."

"What the fuck, Teach," he said. "You got some nerve hanging on. It's just plain selfish what you're putting your kids through, watching you die a little every day."

"They will probably hate me for a while after I'm gone," I said. "Maybe even think I've ruined their life by dying." I swear a slight wince crossed Buddy's face as I spoke, his fleeting second of acknowledgement to me and to the truth.

He pulled his cap off and the red strands of hair became an inferno. Five fingers with half-bitten nails tore through his hair. Buddy Baker had no lifelines—no Victor, no Jack, no Kathy Emerald, no Grandpa Joe to steer him clear of the storm raging inside. His darkness prevailed, nurtured by an abusive father and Leg Iron Baker. We faced each other across an abyss of time; we both knew pain, and the same, but different, loss.

"Oh my Lord," Ruby's voice ripped the silence. "Look what you've done to Willy."

Our heads turned. Willy Wu's eyes were downcast, an expanding wetness moved across his groin, down his left leg and onto the floor.

"You scared that poor boy with your foul-mouthed talk," she said.

"Shut the fuck up!" Buddy said. "I didn't do shit to Willy. That bitching of yours has got to stop. I'm going to fix your fat ass. I'm going to shut you up for good."

Ruby seemed to have forgotten that Buddy had tried to strangle her. She appeared to be concerned only for Willy, her *lamb*.

"I am not afraid of you, boy," she rooted herself in front of Buddy. "I wasn't before, and I am not now. Maybe you get some perverted pleasure out of harassing a young woman with breast cancer and from preventing innocent Willy from going to the bathroom, but you don't fool me none. People like you prey on the weak." Ruby put her shoulders back and smoothed her dress. "You want to kill me, boy, than go ahead. It doesn't matter because at my age death is a given. I've tallied up all my sunrises and sunsets, and I thank the good Lord every day for another and another."

Buddy seemed to have developed a twitch or an involuntary tic in his eye.

"I do believe, Buddy," Ruby said, "that you have seen the last of both."

The defiance in Ruby's voice made Buddy fidget. He put his right hand into his pocket and drew on his cigarette, lips together. One long stream of smoke exited his nose. I saw something ominous in his look.

"Fuck you," he said.

"You got one filthy mouth, boy, but dirty words are the mark of a little mind." Ruby glanced towards Willy and then at Buddy. "I'm going to get Willy a change of clothes and don't try to stop me."

Buddy put his arm out in front of Willy, like the driver of an old Chevy protecting a passenger from sudden stops.

"You're not fucking going anywhere," Buddy said, his arm extended, cigarette burning towards his fingers and the ashes falling into Willy's pee.

"Then *you* get Willy his clothes, and *you* see to it that he gets changed." Ruby tore into Buddy with her words.

"Fuck that," he said. "Fuck you."

Willy started to weep. His chin trembled as if his mandible had been dislocated.

"Don't cry, man," Buddy tried to console Willy. "I'm sorry you're caught up in this, dude, everything's going to be cool. You remember how we used to row together? We had fun, dude. I'm Buddy, man, I'm your friend, just stop crying, okay man, just stop the fucking crying."

Willy used the sleeve of his coat to wipe his nose. He searched Buddy's face with the eyes of a preschooler, trying it seemed, but failing to recognize who he was.

"Boy, I'm done talking to you. Are you going to help Willy or not?" Ruby clucked her tongue. There was no way either of them was going to back down. Buddy took his hand out of his pocket and played with the handcuffs hanging from his belt. They let out a hollow metal tone as Buddy fingered them. Ruby waited for Buddy to answer; there was no scent of a truce.

"I'll get them," I said. Buddy's attention shifted towards me. "I'll get Willy's clothes."

"Nice try, Teach," he said, drawing his cigarette out of his mouth.

"I'm done fucking with all this bullshit. Willy, get me a six-pack of beer."

Willy didn't move.

"Now, man, get it now," Buddy said.

"Don't you do it, Willy." Ruby interrupted and stepped over to Willy to wipe his cheeks with her handkerchief. For a moment confusion played on Buddy's face, as if Ruby's gesture to Willy was foreign to him.

"Back off, old woman," Buddy demanded. "Back off or I'll kill you."

She stayed silent, took Willy's hand, closed his fingers around her hanky and then put her face in close to Buddy. They stared at each other until Ruby turned on her heels, turned her back on Buddy, and strode down aisle three. What made her turn on him despite the warnings and her better judgment, I'll never know.

She was within inches of me when the first shot came. It hit dead center of her back. Buddy fired again, the unseen gun in his pocket. The blast tore a hole in his jacket that left the fabric smoldering, a glint of steel protruded from its burnt edges.

Ruby fell at my feet. For such a big woman, she went down gracefully. Perhaps I was unable to process what was happening, but it seemed that she fell in slow motion, arms and legs rubbery, back arched and her apron pocket suddenly giving birth to Abraham Lincoln Desmond's American flag. The second shot went wide, no mortal blow like the first. I was on my knees next to her, cradling her head when Buddy came and loomed over me, his right hand still in his jacket.

"She dead?" he asked. Her skin was warm and there was a faint pulse in her neck. Looking up at him I saw only the outline of his hair in the harsh ceiling lights.

"No," I said as if Buddy had asked me if the snow had stopped.

The word came off my lips from an automated place in my brain

"I need a beer," he said and walked up to Willy who appeared rooted to his spot.

"If I had a gun, I'd shoot you in the back, Buddy Baker." I stood up, my jacket clattering from its load. He looked back over his shoulder and grinned. "Don't be too sure of me, Buddy," I said. "You don't know what I'm capable of."

He put his hands on Willy's shoulders and turned him with an unsympathetic push towards aisle one. The sound of Willy Wu's shoes echoed throughout the store, his soles scraped the linoleum as if laden with lead.

"Your black bitch friend fucked with me, and now you're starting where she left off. Not very smart on your part, Teach, and in case you haven't noticed, I'm the one with the gun." He held his weapon in both hands, fingers overlapped on its handle, then brought the gun level with his stare and pointed it at me. "I doubt there's a god-damned chance in hell that you've got a piece like this in that tin man's parka of yours. Hell, I bet you don't even have a cell phone." Buddy swung the gun high over his head, laughed and fired.

Aisle three went dark, the long fluorescent tube of light sizzling from the blast. Willy ran back to where we stood, his two arms curled around twelve-packs. Their cold surfaces glistened and the metal caps tap-tapped one against the other. His run was heavy-limbed and labored and left him winded and sweating as he came into view. Buddy moved out in front of Willy. The two collided. His right hand held firm on the gun as he played catcher to his precious beer. Willy was like a steamroller. Unburdened of his cargo he kept coming down aisle three.

I looked at Ruby sprawled on the tiled floor of her beloved Whales Market and back at Willy charging towards me. My adrenaline rush was subsiding, and its departure left my legs feeling hollow. Willy tore past me and got as far as the pancake mixes before Buddy yelled at him to stop. The sudden halt caused Willy to lose his footing and without warning he dropped onto the linoleum.

"Shit, man," Buddy said. "Where the hell do you think you're going?" He popped a top off another bottle of beer.

I watched and waited as the deep amber liquid gushed down his throat.

"Stupid … stupid, stupid, stupid," I found my voice again. "This is just plain stupid. Get on your cell phone and call for an ambulance while there is still some life left in Ruby Desmond."

Buddy lifted the bottle off his lips and some of the contents rolled into the corner of his mouth and down his chin. He swiped the runoff with the back of his hand.

"Don't waste time, Buddy, just do it. Now," I said.

"Your friend is shit out of luck, Teach, and so are you," he said. "There will be no calls for help. Look out the window, Teach, it's a fucking big-ass blizzard, and I've got nothing else to do until the sun comes up. So sit down and shut up." He emphasized his intent with the muzzle of his gun pointed at me.

Willy lay tangled in his wet trousers, his face flushed and empty of his glasses. The frames were half hidden under Ruby's hand, as if she'd known to reach for them as they tumbled to the ground. I lowered myself next to Ruby, drew her head onto my lap and picked up Willy's glasses. The lenses were scratched and one arm was twisted, but I managed to adjust them and called to Willy to come retrieve them.

He turned his brooding face toward me and slid over to his glasses. Buddy was out of sight, and as I watched Willy fuss over his frames, I sensed the weight of the snow building on the roof, pressing down on us until death or morning arrived.

PART III

If the soul's exit could be seen, then death would boast
no nightly news, no sermons and no sorrow.

SIXTEEN

The storm blew blustery walls of snow against Whales Market. Outside, the world I knew had disappeared and the world inside had turned upside down. I'd never been close to a gun going off. The ear-shattering sounds had hung in the air like an unhurried echo. Ruby lay dying, her head angled to one side, a cheek resting on my thigh. There was a recognizable rattle in her throat, like a snake shaking its tail to announce *last call*. Blood oozed from Ruby's ears and nose. Abe's flag had spread itself out underneath her, stars and stripes creating a patriotic deathbed.

My instincts about the dying process were no longer those of a fourteen-year-old teenager. I sensed Ruby's spirit slipping away. I could almost see it beginning to take leave. If only death were so defined, so exact that we could track its departure at the moment the soul flees.

The visitors around my mother's bed had offered her reassurance as she summoned the courage to depart this life. I dropped my head close to Ruby's ear and sought to comfort her by singing the bedtime lullaby I made up to put my children to sleep.

Go to sleep said the Moon go to sleep. Close your eyes said the Moon close your eyes. It's time to turn off my light and time to say good night. I love you said the Moon, I love you said the Moon and that makes everything … all right.

There was consolation in the lyrics that soothed crying babies and restless toddlers, and I hoped the same words would assist Ruby as she crossed over.

Willy came and crouched next to us, his glasses tilted on his nose, making one eye seem larger than the other. He had his hand over his mouth, Ruby's hanky stark white between his fingers.

"Sleeping," he said.

"Not yet," I answered, "but soon."

Music came from his throat. How could Mrs. Wulinsky's son know the tune to my lullaby? The timbre of his humming had the quality of a harp and together our duet rose up like mourners praying the rosary, higher and higher, in hopes that God would hear and put an end to suffering.

Buddy opened another bottle of beer and quickly swallowed the contents. "Enough bullshit," he said, bringing his hand down onto Willy's back and pulling him up by his shirt. Willy stumbled but Buddy hung on until Willy was on his feet.

"Put your arm out," Buddy commanded. Willy raised his left arm as if to ask a question and Buddy clasped a handcuff onto his wrist. A look of astonishment crossed Willy's face as he stared at the silver bracelet on his forearm, its loose twin dangling free. Buddy pushed Willy Wu against the hard-sugar decorations, and a few fell onto the floor. He stepped over to me, crushing several *Happy Birthdays* under his boots. Holding onto Willy's wrist, Buddy reached down and yanked my right arm up to meet Willy's left one.

Click.

"I'm fixing things so nobody goes anywhere," Buddy said with a callous grin. He pushed Ruby onto her back with his foot. Her left arm flopped hard onto the floor. Her body, now sunny-side up, appeared to be sleeping. Leg Iron Baker's grandson laughed as he maneuvered between the three of us, and with a series of quick movements, he wrested Ruby's right arm out from under her and attached the second pair of handcuffs to her and to me.

Once adamant about not believing in the power of prayer, I began to search the dusty files of rote memory for a short entreaty that would save us. I opened and closed my eyes, trying to ease the feeling of terror that had arrived.

Buddy's cell phone blurted its harsh thumping ring. It jolted me back into the present and forced me to acknowledge a different kind of despair, the kind that newspapers print under blurry front-page photographs in the aftermath of tragedy. I continued to question my former loss of hope as Buddy reached inside his jacket for his telephone. If prayer was the answer, I was a rank amateur. Ruby mumbled something unintelligible and Willy crouched and started to move sideways along the aisle.

I thought of Jack asleep at his mother's, alone in the maple-wood bed of his youth. I could see his slumber, the rise and fall of his chest, and hear his soft snores.

I knew nothing about telepathy, but the voice inside me pleaded for him to wake up. Perhaps I could conjure a link, a mental wave of energy that would cause him to open his eyes. Oh God, I prayed, give me the power to get my husband, his horses and all of his men down here to Whales to put us all back together again.

Willy had moved past the cake mixes and the puddings. I started to feel my body sliding along the floor. My right arm was extended straight out and I maneuvered along the tiles as best I could, hoping he would stop soon.

"Willy …" I whispered, "Willy … Stop, please."

Buddy remained distracted and unaware of Willy's travel.

"Listen, I'm getting beer and butts at Whales, I got some stuff to do before I get to your place, so just chill until I get there," Buddy said. He talked with his back turned, a cigarette held deftly between two fingers. Willy kept on his course, dragging Ruby and me to someplace other than aisle three. My right arm started to ache. I didn't know why Buddy didn't hear the grate of bodies and shoes. He was talking about Diane to the unseen caller, and the conversation made him deaf to his surroundings.

"No, man, Diane's not coming. She's tied up." Buddy laughed. "Did I say something funny, dude?" Buddy said. "Yeah, man, I'm a regular fucking stand-up comic."

The caller kept his attention and it wasn't until Ruby's foot got caught up in the pile of fallen groceries that Buddy turned. He was standing sideways and saw our receding procession through the corner of his eye.

"What the fuck?" He shook his head in disbelief. "Hey, man, I got some pain-in-the-ass shit to deal with here, so I'll call you back." He hung up.

"Fucking Willy," he said. "Hey, dude, where the fuck do you think you're going?"

Willy stopped, maybe perplexed by Buddy's questions, maybe tired, or maybe scared. He put the brakes on, and the chain of Buddy's three musketeer hostages undulated.

"Sit down, dude," Buddy ordered. "Sit the fuck down." Willy dropped like he'd been shot. My arm smacked against his and the handcuff rubbed the bone around the base of my thumb. Ruby's short escape left a trail of blood, smudged wide and jagged along the floor. Buddy stepped onto it leaving boot prints as he made his way down to us.

"The two of you," Buddy pointed his cigarette at the shortening and oil shelf, "get back up against there." Willy and I exchanged a glance and pushed off on our palms to do as Buddy directed. Ruby was diagonal in the aisle. "This bitch is still pissing me off."

With the toe of his boot, Buddy punted two boxes of double fudge brownie mix to the top of the aisle and as if just warming up he kicked another and then without warning his boot was in the air again, but this time the blow came down between Ruby and me. The full force of Buddy's kick connected with my lower left arm. I heard something crack and wondered if he had broken his foot, but then a wave of pain went up my arm, so vehement that I leaned over and threw up. Tea and cookies, which had melded together into an alien mass, spilled out of my mouth.

"What the fuck, Teach." Buddy said.

"My arm ..." I heaved again. "It's broken."

"Tough shit," Buddy said. "That's what you get for hanging out with that mother-fucking bitch." I lifted my right hand, taking Willy's left hand with me, and tried to wipe the bile off my chin. Willy Wu, his right hand free and still bearing Ruby's hanky, leaned toward me and cleaned my face.

"Thanks," I said, trying to take in more oxygen. The room was spinning. I let Willy continue. He used the handkerchief like a mother cat's tongue, wiping my chin, my lips, and the tip of my nose and under my neck. If I passed out and went into shock, it might all be over. Breaking my arm could be the exit, a way to call a halt to the madness. Without me to mock, Buddy had no enemy. He was leaning against the brownie mixes with an arrogant expression of pleasure on his face. I tried to lift my left shoulder. The effort made me yelp. Buddy's face broke out into a broad smile.

"Oh, poor teacher is really fucked." Buddy spoke in a singsong voice. He repeated the phrase over and over as if he were reciting a nursery rhyme, and then added, "Kill the teacher. Kill the teacher." He produced from his pocket the gun that shot Ruby. "See this, Teach?" Buddy asked. "This here is a beautiful piece. If I shoot you with it, then, counting the old lady, that'll make three people in one night."

Buddy Baker was working his old game with me, sticking his skewer of ridicule deep into my belly and then watching me thrash

about as he thrust it deeper and deeper. I looked at him and held his
stare. If he was trying to break me, then he'd gotten a good start, but
if he meant to kill me, then he'd met his match. Almost twenty-four
hours ago I'd wanted to die. If Buddy had rung my doorbell yesterday,
waving his gun at me, I would have begged him to shoot me.

Our eyes remained locked. Who would look away first? Something
inside me fanned a flame that had almost been extinguished. No,
Buddy, I am not going to be number three, I thought, but who was
number one? Was it Diane? The question sat on the inside of my
closed lips. If I blurted out my curiosity with too much interest,
Buddy might misinterpret.

He crossed his arms and tipped backward so his hair spread
against an array of boxed, low-carb muffins. His attention was
wavering. Buddy Baker's eyes began to dart past mine, then back
again. Soon each momentary look away became longer until he
forgot me altogether. He got up and walked to the front door. He
turned the lock, then went to the back of the store and started to
play with the switches. One by one he dimmed or shut off each light
fixture in Whales Market.

Buddy found the sound system and spun through the channels,
getting mostly static. He settled on a country-western station whose
middle-of-the-night tunes were deep into unrequited love ballads.
The volume got turned up, and Buddy sang along with the plucking
of grief-stricken guitars. His voice wasn't bad, and he'd nearly
mastered that *twang* which is critical to making listeners cry. He
came across the main aisle at the front of the store with his hands
and arms working imaginary strings on a guitar. Buddy played his
invisible instrument and moved his feet to the rhythm of country
crooning.

There were few commercials, and the ones that made it to my ears
were for beer and fast cars. The announcer spoke about the weather

in sentences strung together with the same intonation as Buddy's karaoke imitation. Willy continued to minister to Ruby and me, reaching over to pat her forehead or slide the hanky along her cheek. With his face so close to mine I could see a growth of stubble on his jaw. Odd how I hadn't associated Willy Wu with the mundane task of shaving. Buddy returned to aisle three, glanced in our direction and seemed satisfied that we were still where he left us.

"I'm hungry," he announced opening another beer. "Willy," he said shaking his head in exasperation, "quit fucking around dude." Willy Wu understood and stopped wiping Ruby's face.

Over the next hour, Buddy scouted the aisles, filling a hand basket with assorted fast foods, dessert snacks and candy bars, coming back intermittently for another beer. I had no idea when Willy had eaten supper, but I was sure that he was hungry too.

"Buddy," it took a few seconds to raise my voice, to get it steady and commanding, "bring Willy something to eat." A freezer door opened with a loud *pop* of suction and closed with a pronounced *whoosh*. His narrow heeled boots resonated with each step he took and cellophane crinkled from bags of potato chips, pretzels and corn chips squashed end to end. Buddy made no reply to my request. Instead he came up Willy's end of the aisle and handed him a tonic and some éclairs. Willy Wu gulped down the beverage and licked off the chocolate icing from his pastry.

"Thanks, Buddy," I said, keeping eye contact with him. He had finished off several more bottles of beer along with whatever food he scavenged from throughout the store. His gun was out of sight.

"Want anything else, man?" Buddy asked Willy. "There's some ass-kicking frozen pizza in aisle four."

Willy had a layer of frosting on his upper lip. His tongue flicked in and out of his mouth, transporting the sweet topping to his taste buds, and at the mention of pizza his face brightened.

"Pizza," Willy said, smiling, the shiny chocolate surface spreading out towards his ears and under his nose.

"And you, Teach?" Buddy said to me. "I do believe I should whip you up an unforgettable *last meal*." His deep-set eyes danced and twirled.

"I'll pass," I said.

"No such luck, Teach," Buddy said. "You can't turn down genuine hospitality. It isn't polite." He mocked me by adding a nasal quality to his voice and then grew agitated waiting for me to answer. The alcohol in his system inflamed his cheeks and reduced his usual swagger to an unsteady lurch.

"I want to speak with you, Buddy." I took in an extra breath. "When you finish getting pizza for Willy, we can talk." It took him a few seconds to absorb my words. This wasn't what he was expecting to hear, not the answer to his offer of a last supper.

"You're fucking unbelievable, Teach," Buddy said, holding a fresh beer in one hand and a newly lit cigarette in the other. "Look at you, tied to the fucking cross and still giving orders. Piss off, Teach, because I say when we talk and when we eat, when you live and when you die." He turned on his heels and stumbled up the aisle. Suddenly he swung around and used his beer as a pointer towards Willy Wu.

"Stay put," he said. "I like you too much, dude, don't do anything stupid, okay?"

Willy Wu nodded.

"Because next time, dude, I'll have to shoot you." Buddy belched and disappeared down aisle four.

SEVENTEEN

I heard Buddy rummage through the freezer section and then followed his footsteps to the small room we had occupied earlier in the evening. There was a clatter of dishes, a shattering of china, and I imagined Ruby's wedding teacups succumbing to Buddy's impatience. He must have moved past the bits and pieces to the microwave because I heard its familiar beep, and seconds later the drone of a late-night talk show came from the television. Hollywood sarcasm now vied with lost love on the radio. I looked at Willy. He was struggling to keep his eyes open.

"Close your eyes, Willy," I said. "Get some sleep until Buddy comes back." Willy Wu's lids fluttered, and within seconds his breathing was mixed with faint snores. I was exhausted. My left arm screamed at me, but I couldn't allow myself to listen. There were too many other screeches coming from my body, all of them bouncing off each other in an effort to be quelled. I rested my head back and took a deep breath. There was nothing I could do but try and talk to Buddy. My voice was my only weapon, my only means of defense. I closed my eyes for a short while to refortify myself for the confrontation ahead, and without conscious effort I fell asleep.

No trees were down or children running to catch the ice-cream man in the dark corridor between waking and sleep. This dream took me to a field where I was buried up to my neck. I was a head growing out of a graveyard of weeds, abandoned cars, tires and rubble. A small hut appeared in the distance. If I twisted my neck to the left, I could see a single bulb burning through a window without glass, a curtain blowing in the breeze. The "curtain" was two pairs of jeans, the legs flapping, overlapping, outside and inside the window. A hooded specter passed across the stark light. Something in its grasp rose and fell, up and down, up and down with unrelenting force. An animal shrieked after each blow, and in the after-silence, a noise echoed like claws across concrete.

The sinister figure reached for a dangling pull chain. All went black. In the darkness and without vision, I was more vulnerable, more victim. What skulked? What waited to pounce? I felt a presence and heard panting, quick intakes and expulsions of air. The beaten animal was at my neck sending out a hot moist spray, and I, devoid of all except instinct, knew its need for revenge.

I opened my eyes and Buddy Baker was an inch from my face. His breath smelled rancid with beer. My jaw was slack from sleep and before I could swallow or run my tongue over dry lips, Buddy shoved a steaming piece of pizza between them. His left hand clamped onto the back of my head while the other held tight to the pizza so I couldn't resist. The cheese and sauce scorched my palate and gums. All the howls inside my body merged together. Tears came but were ineffective and had no access to the burning interior of my mouth. They only gave Buddy greater satisfaction. He held me in a vise-grip, working the blistering heat of the dough against my tongue, sending a clear message that I should *shut up*.

"So you want to talk, huh, Teach?" Buddy said. "Try and talk now, just try. I'm the boss, you hear? I'm the boss. Fuck you."

He yanked the slice of pizza out of my mouth and threw it against a display of smiley faces and clown party hats. My lips and tongue began to swell and painful mounds of seared tissue surrounded my teeth.

Breast cancer and Buddy Baker were one and the same, both

trying to suck me down. Yesterday, I gave in to cancer, gave myself over to a disease that had taken me into the bowels of despair, into the belly of hell; a disease that had no sympathy, no compassion and no purpose other than to kill me. Now I was confronted by Buddy, a black-hooded murderer, another kind of killer who had taken me hostage, who had no mercy, no kindness and no other purpose than to take my life. Buddy and cancer wanted a sign, wanted me to concede my battle with each, to fly the flag of defeat.

I glared at him. I would not surrender to either.

Buddy backed off. Momentarily defused, he reached for another piece of pizza and gave it to Willy. Buddy and Willy Wu spent several minutes intent on eating. The noise of their chewing blended with the chords of a Texas two-step. Another can of tonic was passed to Willy, and Buddy drank more beer. The meal provided by Buddy included an ice cream cake with blue and green icing and flowers cascading down one corner. When the pizza was gone, Buddy opened a switchblade attached to his key ring and cut generous pieces of the cake for him and Willy Wu. He used a package of plates and one of napkins from the few remaining on the shelf, opening each with his teeth.

They lifted mounds of cake to their lips on tiny plastic forks. I watched them, all the time thinking of Annalise's cupcakes, thawed and unfrosted, waiting for me on the kitchen counter. My mind scanned the rest of the rooms of my house, peering into doorways like a ghost. Ten Nettles Cove. I wanted to get back there, wished I'd never left, and prayed in an out-of-practice voice for a miracle.

"Who is Diane?" I said. The words were slurred, my fat tongue unable to get out of its own way.

Willy paused to look at me. Ice cream melted on his lips. It slid around the crumbs of cake crust that lined the corners of his mouth and ran down his chin. Only his eyes moved, going from me to Buddy.

"What the fuck, Teach?" Buddy said. "You don't quit, do you?" He jabbed his fork into the last piece of cake. The slender plastic handle vibrated even after Buddy's hand moved away.

"Diane's dead," he said. "Dead because she couldn't keep her mouth shut. Kind of like you, Teach, always preaching, always something to say. She didn't know when to be quiet, fucking bitch, always had to have the last word."

Buddy didn't look at me when he spoke. He talked to a person Willy and I couldn't see, a presence neither of us wanted to meet. His index finger passed over the top of the plastic handle, back and forth, back and forth, until it snapped, leaving only the imbedded prongs. I waited and watched Buddy's mood change from hostile to maudlin, and back to hostile.

"Where is she?" I asked.

He picked up the end of the fork and held it in his palm, turning it over, as if there was a message along its length. His attention roamed the room, blind to Willy and me.

"Outside," he said. Buddy's answer came from low in his throat, and with that one word a tear escaped and traveled his cheek quickly, as if trying not to be seen. He got up and blew his nose in a wad of birthday napkins, then took one of the few remaining beers from its brightly decorated carton, popped the cap and swallowed hard. His Adam's apple bobbed up and down, up and down, as the liquid flowed down his throat.

"You loved her?" I said.

Buddy didn't look at me. Instead, he stared into his beer bottle.

"Diane's tied up in the bed of my pick-up." The alcohol was so alive in him, so dictating his response, that another tear escaped his eyes. He began to keen, wrapping his arms around himself, swaying. His head was hanging low close to his arms.

"She was going to ..." Buddy garbled his words and caught

himself. "She was splitting. Fucking gonna leave me." He lifted his head backwards. "The whore claimed she didn't want to hurt me. What kind of crap is that? Hurt me? Some broad on a hotline told her to pack her fucking bags and get out." Buddy's eyes were fixed on the ceiling. "*Please*, the little bitch said *please* to me. Wouldn't I try to understand? She loved me but she had to leave."

"What did you say?" I asked.

Buddy didn't look at Willy or me. He continued to make his confession to the overhead fixture.

"I said fuck you bitch, you can't leave." He dropped his arms and the swaying stopped. He ran his fingers through his hair. "Then I back-handed her in the face. Hard enough that her whole body left the floor, her head snapped back and hit the bedroom wall. I think the bitch was dead then. I think I goddamn killed her with one blow, but being so pissed I got my gun and stood over her. She wasn't fucking going anywhere, I told her, fucking ever. That's when I shot her. Then I went and finished off the beers in the fridge and watched some TV. Later, I came here the first time and that black bitch over there," Buddy pointed to Ruby, "that *nigger* wouldn't give me beer."

Ruby moaned. Buddy stiffened. He looked confused by Ruby's sudden show of life. He let out a breath, a deep resonating sigh that told of his pain. But Buddy was a *blamer*, brought up by blamers, and he wouldn't, or couldn't, take responsibility for *why* his girlfriend wanted to leave him. His tears were for himself. The pity and agony were for how ugly and unfair life had been to *him*. Diane deserved what she got, a whack that killed her and a bullet to the brain, which was what she had asked for, according to Buddy.

"I get the short end of the stick all the fucking time," Buddy said. "Like Willy. Yeah, just like Willy. We both got fucked the day we were born."

Willy leaned across me, listening to Buddy. A moment before

he had been nodding in and out of sleep. It must have been the emphatic tone in Buddy's voice when he spoke Willy's name that got his attention.

"You see, Teach, I've got no beef with Willy. Willy and me, we got history. I'd never hurt him. He got caught up in this tonight, but he's just along for the ride. After I shoot you, when it's over, when this whole goddamn mess is over, Willy is going home to sleep in his own bed."

Buddy smiled at Willy and gave him a little wave with his beer bottle. I looked at Willy's profile, the way his lower lip jutted out and nostrils flared as he listened.

"Hey man, did you like the pizza?" Buddy asked. Willy didn't answer and Buddy's forehead furrowed. "The dude doesn't say much, does he?"

"He processes more than we give him credit for," I said. Willy turned almost full face to look at me as I spoke.

"Willy Wu hears," Willy said, his voice steady and sure.

"Fuck, dude, don't listen to Teach's bullshit. She's like Diane, always trying to twist things, always trying to get you to look at both sides of something, the big fucking picture." He threw his legs out in front of him. His boots slapped together with a sharp clatter of heels and hard leather. Buddy tapped his empty bottle on the linoleum. "I need more beer," he said and reached over to the carton to extract the last bottle.

"Willy man, you and me, we gotta stick together. We're kindred spirits, that's what we are. Isn't that right, Teach?" Buddy leveled his eyes upon me. "You like that kind of talk, don't you, Teach? Kindred spirits and all that crap, that's up your alley." Buddy extended his right foot so it connected with mine. He kicked at me. "What happened, Teach, pizza got your tongue?" A loud hoot came out of Buddy. He slapped his knee and laughed. Willy shook his head and bit his lower lip.

"It's all right, Willy," I said, my words barely distinct above Buddy's laughter.

If I didn't believe everything was all right, then how could I convince Willy Wu?

"Did you tell Diane you loved her?" I asked Buddy. He poured more beer down his throat and let out a long *ahhhh* after he swallowed.

"What's love, Teach?" He twirled the beer in his hand, watching it touch his skin. "There's no such thing as love like in the movies. The kind of love that someone is supposed to have for another, the kind that says no matter what or who you are I still love you. Bullshit, Teach, that's just plain bullshit." Buddy sat up and placed his arms monkey-fashion between his legs. "People in real life don't give a shit about anyone but themselves. Narcissistic I think is what you'd call it, Teach." Buddy's lip curled in a smirk. "Do I impress you with my big words, Teach? Hell, one thing you did right was teaching me vocabulary." He chuckled and took another swig of beer.

"Trouble is, Teach, I live in a fucked up part of town with fucked up people who don't understand all those words. Where I come from, you got to talk the talk."

Buddy yawned. "So the answer is *no*. No, I never told Diane I loved her."

"Too bad," I said. "It feels good to tell people you love them."

Buddy's eyes closed. I had to ask him one more question.

"Did you ever tell your mother you loved her?" Foolish or not, I said what I said.

His eyes flipped open like a switch. Buddy sat up, empowered despite his intake of beer. A visible pulsing started at the outside corner of one eye. The rapid thumping forced Buddy's eyelid to shut and he pressed his fingertips against the beating to quell it. He bent forward, took hold of my shoulders and shook me.

"My mamma ain't none of your business. You got no right, Teach, no right. Love isn't something out of one of your textbooks, or one of your self-help psycho bullshit sessions. Maybe you need to ask me about hate. I can tell you some good shit about hate. I fucking hate your superiority and all that comes with it and because I hate it, I am going to *love* pulling the trigger when I shoot you." Buddy gave my shoulders one last shake then fell back against the shelves.

Tears stung my eyes. I forced them back. My vision had doubled, waves of nausea returned. Willy wiped the corner of my right eye with his thumb. His skin was coarse, but his touch was kind. Buddy had closed his eyes and missed Willy's gesture. I had crossed the line with Buddy, but I had to take that chance. His abuse didn't matter. I couldn't let that stop me.

The heaviness of the middle of the night hung over us. There was nothing more to say because the burden of alcohol in Buddy's system had at last won out. His head lolled and his body twitched with the kind of sleep that causes drivers to crash on roads and highways. Willy settled back. His body weight leaned into my right shoulder, and soon the soft timbre of his breathing was in my ear.

I turned to Ruby. Her face was angled upward. There was movement under her eyelids, as if she were reading something on the underside of them.

"Ruby?" I said in a hoarse whisper. "Ruby can you hear me?" She moaned. Her breathing grew more rapid. "How do I get through to your Lord, Ruby?" I looked at her as if she could answer. "It's okay, Ruby. It's okay. Never mind. I'm here with you. Willy is safe right next to me, and the store is fine too." One eye opened and stared at me, the other remained shut.

EIGHTEEN

I stared into Ruby's glassy orb as if it were a crystal ball and wondered if it had retained the power of sight, or if it was just wide and bright for me to view my own reflection.

The snow hadn't slowed and raged outside. Piled high, its presence had created a sense of insulation, like a spun cocoon, and I was inside, a very small me. On the radio station that Buddy had chosen, romance-gone-bad lyrics drifted up and down the aisles. A female singer complained about her old man's drinking and how she missed the simple days before life got hard. I rested my head on the shelf behind me and stared up at the ceiling. What was it that Buddy had seen up there when he made his confession about Diane? There was no writing, no secret code imprinted on the molding.

I closed my eyes and envisioned myself cross-legged, palms resting upward on my knees. My earliest recollection of practicing yoga was from a fear-of-flying course taken several months before Jack and I were married. We were flying to the Fijian Islands for our honeymoon, a journey that would take us thousands of miles over land and sea. At the time, the thought of being in an airplane cruising at an altitude that hid mother earth from sight was unduly frightening.

Whales Market wasn't a plane ride. Our linked bodies couldn't lift off. I took deep diaphragm breaths and wished that none of this had happened, that it wasn't true. I wished and prayed because now I knew that I could survive the act of flying, but I wasn't sure how to save us from going down tonight.

Ruby groaned.

"Let go, Ruby," I said trying to soothe her. "Abe is waiting for you on the other side. He has his hand out. Reach for it, Ruby, and cross over." Her lips moved in a wordless response. "Did you hear Buddy say he wouldn't harm Willy? He's going to let him go after ..."

I couldn't finish my sentence. After what? After he killed me? After the snow stopped? After he drank more beer? Across from me, the toes of his boots touching mine, Buddy slept. The stark truth of our situation continued to bear down on me. There was no one to call for help. The possibility of a rescue was remote. In the waning darkness, I sorted through the reality of what could happen when Buddy woke up

The possibility of being nothing more than a photograph on our mantel or on a side table loomed. I had courted death, waltzed with it and struggled to make peace with it, but now, faced with the ending of my life, death had lost its appeal. Who was I to assume the role of a mystic, urging Ruby to take the mythical ferry across to the other side when I hadn't yet come to grips with my own death? Yesterday, I was in mourning for the old me, the one whom the bald-headed woman in the mirror had replaced. Today that hole in my mirror could be in my chest, put there by a bullet from Buddy Baker's gun.

If that wasn't enough, I was a *hypocrite*. How could I profess to know about love to Buddy when I didn't tell Jack that I loved him yesterday? How could I do that? How could I have opened my eyes yesterday morning and not told Jack Emerald that I loved him back? My heart ached for my family and Ten Nettles Cove. Every person that mattered most to me lived within those walls. I wanted to go there again to feel the softness of the towels hanging on the racks, smell the flowers in our garden when the windows were open and nestle into our bed next to Jack.

Our bed, a wide and generous California King, is an anchor to us, the kids, the dog and anyone else who cares to scramble upon its duvet cover. In happy and sad times, we climb aboard or go under the covers for deep discussions, burying our heads during blackouts and games of hide and seek. Sick or well, our family has always taken refuge in our bed.

Jack and I hurried to our room the night before my mastectomies. We fell on our bed and clung to each other as if the mattress were a great vessel that had been tossed onto the waves of a perfect storm. Our bodies intertwined like vines. We cried and laughed into the wee hours of the morning. One moment we would be buoyed by good memories and the next moment heartbroken by others. We talked, we made love and we talked again. Back and forth we went from our beginnings to our dreams of the future. These reminiscences took us to our wedding, honeymoon and the births of our children.

Four years passed between that first afternoon when Jack and I sat in Grandma Rose's kitchen and the day we became man and wife. We were married the summer I graduated from state teachers' college, the summer I accepted a job in the English department of Gloucester High School. Jack had been doing research at Cape Cod and would begin his own environmental research company that fall. Our wedding guest list was small, the ceremony and celebration intimate. Kathy was my maid of honor, and my brother served as best man. My father lent us his antique car, the one whose name I shared. I thought it was kind of foolish, but Jack knew better. He said that our short ride in Victor's automobile symbolized, for my father, his daughter's traveling from infancy to womanhood.

We drove with the old Hudson's windows rolled down, my veil pouring out, billowing high above the car's roof. Jack had to work the steering wheel hard taking corners. Each time he down-shifted he would turn to me, his mouth wide, full tenor voice bouncing off the grained leather seats as he bellowed a silly song about the car and me. Finally I told him to stop or I was getting out. Jack laughed and I pretended to think he was ridiculous.

If my father's car was our *something borrowed*, then the pearl Jack gave me for my nineteenth birthday was the bridal *something old*. I still wear the necklace, the single pearl on a fine gold chain. It has become my good luck charm along with the headscarf I made from a Fijian souvenir.

Jack and I had browsed an outdoor market in Savusavu during our stay in Fiji. One of the vendors, a brightly dressed woman from one of the outlying villages, had a basket brimming over with decorated pieces of fabric called *sulus*. She let me pick through her selections, patiently explaining some of the history of these island garments. Men and women visitors were encouraged to wear them as a way of displaying respect for the customs of her people.

Jack's choice had a vivid blue background and mine was red with sprays of budding flowers. Red represents power, the island woman told me, and the flowers symbolize hope. Little did I know that years later I would wear the same cloth wrapped around my naked scalp.

Our trip to the South Pacific was unforgettable. Jack hired a small boat, captained by a clever New Zealander named Ted, who picked us up each morning and dropped us at a different atoll everyday. We were on specks of sand in a vast ocean where Jack could set up his tripod and comb through the wonders of the marine environment. Sometimes Ted would anchor offshore, and he and Jack would dive the brilliant coral reefs. On those days, I would swim to shore and find a secluded spot to shed my bikini top and sunbathe. My skin turned the color of brown sugar and my breasts became bronzed. Like a sea nymph, I splashed along each shore, and when I floated on my back, the froth of the ocean's movement churned against my nipples, coaxing them to rise above the water's rim and point towards the sun.

Those same breasts later nursed four babies, including my twins. I had read that nursed infants were healthier than bottle-fed ones, and that mothers who breast-fed were less likely to develop breast cancer.

I asked Dr. Hammer if my topless sunbathing had contributed to my disease. He smiled his perfect white smile and shook his head. He did not advocate exposing any skin to the sun. He said this while pushing back a stray lock of his hair with tanned fingers, but it was unlikely that my particular cancer stemmed from that exposure. What about nursing? Didn't that count for something, I asked him?

"Yes," he had said, "yes, I'm sure it does for many women." He further explained that although studies or data were not clear on the benefits or the guarantees for preventing cancer, nursing most certainly was a positive for some mothers.

I saw and heard this as more of his doubletalk. As Jack and I lay together the night before my surgery, I wept for my breasts. I cried like a discarded lover for the coming absence of a *whole* body. Jack's tears mixed with mine, but his sorrow was for the possible tomorrows set to be stolen from us. My husband could not imagine growing old without me by his side. All the hopes and wishes that lay ahead were wrapped inside *our* life.

The next morning we gathered at the kitchen table with the children and had a family meeting. The boys understood the gravity of the situation but it was Annalise who spoke. She came and stood by my chair. Her small fingers played with my hair, twirling it around and around. When Jack finished, she looked up at me and said, "Don't be scared, Mummy. Nighttime scary things are just your stuffed animals in the morning."

Jack stayed with me as long as he could before the operation. He told me funny stories about sea creatures and trivia he had read in the newspaper. When the anesthesiologist came to speak to me, I made a wisecrack about his clogs, but the doctor didn't laugh. I told Jack I thought the man was a stiff, and Jack said no, Hud, when the doctor puts you to sleep, he wants you to wake up again. He's serious because anesthesia is serious.

My husband is so wise in the most simplistic of ways. In the days post surgery, Jack was always there. He slept in my room. Even with my eyes closed, I could sense his presence, could smell the sweet scent of his skin.

I inhaled, hoping for that powdered aroma, but the dank, fetid smell of urine rose to my nostrils. Willy had wet himself again. Oh God, I thought, I needed to thrust myself back to where my mind had been at Ten Nettles Cove, but Jack's face faded, and the comfort of his voice was going too. His secure embrace fell away, leaving me propped up between Ruby Desmond and Willy Wu.

The back of my head ached from resting on the edge of the shelf. Instinct prompted me to rub it but I couldn't. I attempted to shift my hips without disturbing Willy or Ruby, but as I lifted my head and tried rocking gently to give my bottom some relief, Buddy's cell phone rang. The sound jolted me out from under Willy, sending my good arm straight in front of me. Buddy reacted, too. His boots slammed into my shins, forcing me to jerk even further forward, sending poor Ruby's head onto my lap. Willy was thrown to the right. He looked around with a dazed expression, as if he couldn't comprehend or recognize his surroundings. Awakened from a deep sleep, a part of his brain appeared to have erased the nightmare of Whales Market. Willy started to make a high-pitched noise. The sound came from the back of his throat, a neighing that rose octave upon octave until its pitch was painful to my ears. *Neigh* ... it cut through the radio's music. *Neigh* ... it covered the television's talk. It drowned out even Buddy's cell phone ring tone.

Buddy slid across the floor to Willy, using his elbow as a lever.

"Hey man, hey Willy." Buddy at first remained calm, but Willy did not have the capacity for reason. "Shut him up!" Buddy said to me. "Shut him the fuck up, or I'm going to smack him good."

My thoughts were of Diane, dead from one of Buddy's blows. I stroked Willy's leg, drenched in his fresh wetness. His hand, cuffed to mine, followed my fingers. Willy's neighs finally turned to whimpers, and then he was silent. He put his free hand on top of mine and gave it a squeeze. I smiled at him and he at me. Buddy had let the call go without answering. He went off to aisle one instead. We could hear him opening and closing the cooler. When he came back, Buddy stood at the end of our aisle. He stretched his arms above his head, one hand wrapped around a cold bottle of beer. Willy and I watched him rub his eyes and bite his fingernails. He drank his beer as if it were his morning cup of black coffee. The phone rang again.

This time Buddy took the call. He turned his back on us and walked towards the cash register. His voice was low and, except for a few expletives, I couldn't catch what he was saying. The drawer of the register opened, and I heard loose change hitting the floor and skidding off under the counter. One more affront to add to all the others. Buddy was retrieving his money. He slammed the drawer and went back to use the restroom. Then he returned to Ruby's kitchen where the volume on the television was high enough that we could hear the incongruous sound of canned laughter.

Willy held my hand, but his attention had shifted to Ruby. He took his hand off mine and reached over to her. He ran the tips of his fingers along her hairline. There were tears in Willy's eyes. It was odd how I didn't think he was capable of that kind of emotion. His head drooped and his shoulders caved in to sadness. I was relieved that Buddy was out of sight, thankful that Willy could grieve in peace.

NINETEEN

Ruby's breathing could not be heard over the radio and the television. There was nothing to say at a time like this. I picked up our joined wrists and once again patted Willy's leg. My voice choked in my throat. He started rocking and his sobs turned to hiccups. His nose began to run. A pile of napkins with big, round clown faces lay close to his feet. I pointed and he leaned over to retrieve them. Willy pulled out a few and wiped my face.

"Take care of you, Willy," I said, and he stopped, perhaps for a moment unsure of what I meant. In the seconds that he hesitated, the fluids running down his face congealed under his lip. Willy brought the birthday napkins to his chin as if he were catching a bug. He took a tight hold of the sticky pool with a wad of paper clowns, and out of the crumbled layers they grinned back at me.

Ruby stirred. She was on her side, her right arm twisted upward across her body attached to mine like a corkscrew. A violent shudder ran along its length. My arm, dangling useless between us, moved with the quake. Her voice rose from her throat in a sudden clear *Alleluia*. Then silence. Her suffering was over. She was gone, leaving behind her old woman's body like an empty conch shell on the beach.

The stillness she left gave consolation. Droning guitars and re-runs receded in death's presence. The Grim Reaper had sat down with us like a vulture drawn to the scent of death. If Buddy had his way, the next to go would be me.

"Willy," I leaned as close to him as our cuffed arms would allow. "Let's say a prayer for Ruby's soul," I said. He raised only his eyes. "Do you know a prayer we can say?" I asked. He shook his head. "We can make one up," I said. "We can say a prayer of our own that is just for Ruby, our friend. Okay?"

Willy nodded in agreement. He moved his free hand to meet the one tethered to mine and put his palms together. Willy made a flat tent with his fingers and crossed his thumbs. The prayer was up to me.

"Well, here goes nothing," I said and began to pray. "This prayer is to Ruby Desmond's Lord. Willy Wu and I hope that you are listening. Ruby Desmond was a good woman, and our world has an empty space in it now that she is gone. Willy and I will miss her kindness and her generosity. Please keep the lights on in heaven so her son, Abe, can find his way home." Willy sat up when I began our prayer and rested his face on the tips of his fingers. He listened with his mouth opened slightly, his tongue visibly working through the words and their meanings. When I got to the part about Abe he looked over at the flag unfurled under Ruby. That was when the prayer ended. I skipped the Amen part.

How long Willy and I sat there I do not know. It seemed like hours. Neither of us moved, we just stayed quiet, each of us lost in our own thoughts. Buddy must have fallen asleep again. Maybe he would sleep well into the morning, long enough for the sun to rise and customers to come for their coffee and newspaper. But just as I entertained that possibility, I heard his boots stamp on the floor above us. A toilet flushed, and his heavy-footed steps resonated through the rooms overhead. Willy stretched his neck upward.

"Bad man," he said.

"Yes," I whispered, "a very bad man." Doors opened and closed and something was thrown on the floor then dragged around as Buddy walked. I had a mental picture of Buddy loading up a duffle bag, maybe one that belonged to Abe, with knick-knacks, silverware and candle sticks. I had no idea what sort of treasures Ruby Desmond had in her home above Whales Market, but I knew that Buddy was on the prowl, and anything that glittered or required a battery would catch his attention. Buddy Baker was bored and that wasn't a good sign.

"Willy," I said. "Can you do me a favor?" He was still looking up at the ceiling as if he could track Buddy's footsteps. "Willy, please I need you to do me a favor. We're friends, right?"

I pulled on his hand. Several more seconds elapsed before Willy withdrew his attention from the echo of Buddy's footsteps. He searched my face with his eyes, making me wonder about my appearance and about how frightening the woman in the mirror looked yesterday, and how that same woman had morphed even further into an object of repulsion. His expression did not seem concerned about my exterior; it held instead an open question mark drawn across his forehead and down his face.

"Okay, Willy, listen. We have to figure out how we can escape from Buddy. I need you to concentrate on helping me create a plan, quickly," I said.

He didn't answer. I did not expect him to reply right away. My request, I knew, was sinking down through his filter system, down into an unknown place to be processed. The gloom of our predicament increased as his mind churned over the idea of fleeing. There were few options available. We had no key to our handcuffs, and with Ruby dead, her body had turned into two hundred pounds of anchor. I scanned aisle three and remembered what was still in my pockets. All the hours that had passed and I still wore Jack's ski jacket filled with party supplies. A few sections down from Willy was a display of cake cutters, serving pieces and knives. It would be absurd to think we could cut through steel, but maybe we could wrestle Buddy down and get his gun. Usually so resourceful, I kept coming up blank. I sighed. A deep frustrating sound came out of my mouth.

None of that would work.

I was kidding myself into believing that I wouldn't be just another ninety pounds of anchor. It didn't matter that Willy was stumped for an answer to my request. The only real favor he could effectively complete for me was not to die. One of us had to survive, and whatever happened, Willy Wu needed to come out of this alive, for his sake and for mine.

"Never mind, Willy," I said. "There is nothing we can do." As my words entered the space between us, a series of loud thuds came from upstairs and then down. Buddy was throwing things off the stairwell from Ruby's apartment. Willy tried to stand up. He got almost to his feet and then remembered Ruby and me. I tried to slide up on my knees, but fresh movement to my broken arm renewed its throbbing

"There's nothing we can do, Willy," I repeated. "Sit down before Buddy comes back." Getting Buddy more upset was not going to keep Willy alive, but he wouldn't sit down. He reached for a box of cake mix and threw it up the length of the aisle.

"Stop, Willy," I said, but after the first box, he threw another and another. When the cake mixes were all gone, he grabbed pudding, napkins and plates. Soon a pile formed at the end of the aisle like the foundation of a fortress. This was Willy's answer, his defense against the *bad man*. I knew it wouldn't be too long before Buddy came back. Whatever he was accumulating at the foot of Ruby's stairs couldn't compare with what Willy had begun to build.

The noise stopped and we heard Buddy's two feet hit the floor of the back room. He must have had to leap over his booty to get past it. Within seconds he was standing at the end of aisle three, he and

Willy looking like misfits out of a western B-movie.

"What the hell are you doing, dude?" Buddy asked.

But Willy had only stopped long enough to grab a handful of pre-mixed frosting in little cans. He pelted Buddy with them, some hitting their mark others missing and rolling to the floor. Buddy seemed amused by Willy's actions. He moved side to side like a goalie, hand poised for catching, and body for dodging. This game continued for a few minutes until Willy ran out of ammunition and stood, at last, with his hand by his side breathing hard.

"Hey, Willy, you fucking finished, man?" Buddy said. He stepped over the assorted goods and paper products and made his way down to us. "Did anyone ever tell you that you got a good pitching arm, dude?"

He didn't wait for an answer, didn't want an answer. With one motion he shoved Willy down to the floor. He put one booted foot on Willy's groin. "Don't play with me." His boot rotated against Willy's pants. "I can get mean, man, so don't play with me." He lifted his foot and slammed it into the floor making his point. "I'm fucking tired of this whole mess." Buddy backed up a few steps towards the shelves. He used them as back support to slide himself down into a crouch.

"You three can't be trusted," he said, never noticing that Ruby had died. "So I'm back to babysitting you." He stared at his gun, rolling the short barrel in one palm. "Well, I'm done looking at your fucked up faces."

He fixed his gaze on me. All his anger at God, his father, his mother, Diane and whoever else had wronged him, was compressed into his stare. I could feel heat emanating from the whites of his eyes.

"I'm going to kill you. I'm going to get it over with now," Buddy said to me. "I'm going to take this gun and point it at your heart and shoot." His eyes danced around in his head like pinballs in a summer arcade game.

"We've been at this too long. Willy and I need to go home. But you, Teach, you can't go home because you talk too much, you ask too many questions, you're too fucking smart for your own good. Besides, who wants to sit around and watch you croak of cancer, it'll be a mercy killing." He smiled at me, and this time he let his upper lip rise high, and there, for the first time, I saw a row of rotting teeth, their decay worn like a badge of honor.

"Anyway, Teach, you want to die, that's what tonight is about. That black bitch, you and Diane, all three egging me on to kill, to do the Lord's work." He laughed. It struck him so funny that he laughed long and hard until he had to hold his side from the pain of laughing.

Knock. Knock.

Hudson Catalina, God will see you now. God? Was there a heaven or a hell? I didn't know. I hadn't figured it out yet. I was a captive in Whales Market, how absurd, but the horror of Buddy's laughter was real, and I thought if Ruby Desmond's Lord was looking down, then perhaps He would understand if I said I wasn't ready to accept my fate. There would be no last rite alleluias. My mother was not holding out her hand to guide me to the next life. If anything, Anna O'Malley Catalina was telling me it wasn't my time.

"It's not my time, Buddy," I said. He snapped back into his pose, resumed his hold on his gun and leaned back with a slight movement of his feet. "If you kill me, you have not done anyone a favor, least of all yourself. Maybe you should think about why you really want to kill me."

"There you go, Teach, scorched tongue still wagging," he said. "The only way I can get you to shut up is to fucking pull this trigger." He came back up on his toes and leaned into his knees. "You can't talk your way out of this one, Teach."

Anna O'Malley, Anna O'Malley, I said my mother's name over and over like a prayer. Is this the end? Dearest Anna, if this is my demise, please watch over my children and Jack Emerald. Somehow, someway, please give me a sign. I closed my eyes knowing that Buddy's finger was on the trigger.

Willy spoke up.

"Don't point," Willy said to Buddy. "Down," he said, "put it down."

I opened my eyes. Buddy still pointed the gun at me, but he was looking at Willy.

"Man, I told you before that I wouldn't shoot you. I promised you if you didn't screw up I wouldn't shoot you, and I meant it. Willy man, none of this is your fault. Something got real messed up when you were born and besides, we spent too much time together, dude, to let this shit get between us. I got no reason to kill you, man." Buddy muttered the last *kill you, man,* a few times over.

"Friend ..." Willy said.

"Hey man, that's right, I'm your friend, your rowing amigo. Give me five." Buddy offered Willy his fingers spread wide and upright to slap palms, but Willy didn't raise his hand or acknowledge the intended exchange. He took his glasses off and put them back on with one successive action. His lips moved but no sound came out. I strained to catch what Willy wanted to say. As if he could read my mind, he turned towards me.

"Friend ..." he said and looked at me. His lips curled as if waiting for more words to reach them and join *friend* in a complete sentence.

"Cut the bullshit, Willy. She wants to die and you're just slowing down the process with your friend crap." Buddy put both hands around the gun and leaned forward on his haunches. The smell of booze was over me like sour milk. I stared back at him, my eyes wide.

"Don't do it ..." I said.

He snickered.

I felt a slam against my mid-section, followed by agonizing pain and a massive weight on my chest. Warm liquid poured over me like bath water. My eyes had closed and the impact thrust me nearly flat onto the floor. I couldn't breathe. The pressure on my chest was suffocating. I gasped for air. Before I opened my eyes, Buddy let out a wail.

Willy Wu lay on top of me, his head butted up against mine and his body sprawled across me in a dead man's embrace. His pupils were wide and unseeing. Buddy Baker yelped like a dog in the background. He screamed Willy's name.

Willy had flung himself over me. He had put himself in the path of Buddy's bullet.

I felt faint, my arms and legs tingled. My whole body shook. A deep freeze exploded inside me. The bullet couldn't have gone through Willy into me, but why did I feel so cold? Shock. It had to be shock.

My right arm was pressed out to the side against Willy's left, our bodies entwined in a duet of death. Somehow Willy knew to keep my arm free so that when he fell, his arms were spread like wings. Willy knew about heroes.

Buddy dove on top of us. He clawed Willy's arms and pounded his back. I craned my neck to see around Willy's body, but he had me covered completely.

"Goddamn teacher, she made me kill you, Willy. She fucking made me kill you, dude."

Willy was dead weight and Buddy struggled. His feet slipped from under him and coins rolled onto the floor. He swore trying to get his balance and then I heard the soft thump of his wallet and the clunk of his gun as both fell from his pocket. Buddy was so intent on Willy that he didn't hear either drop. He managed to get the key to the handcuffs and unlocked Willy and me. Buddy's fingers encircled my wrist and did a quick search for a pulse, then with two arms around Willy, Buddy drew him backward.

"Oh God, man." Buddy lost his footing again. He and Willy went down against the shelves, which collapsed in a loud roar, a jumble of arms and legs among the metal and screws. What was stacked on each shelf tumbled onto the floor, joining what had been emptied from Buddy's jacket. Several seconds passed before Buddy moved. Howling with misery, he half-carried, half-dragged Willy to the end of aisle three.

PART IV

Jack like the bean stalk,
Emerald like your eyes ...

TWENTY

My right arm was free. I moved it out slowly through the blood and around the debris from Buddy's pockets. Pulse or no pulse, I'm not dead yet, I thought. Turning my head to the right to view my arm's progress, I saw the glint of metal just within my reach. I inhaled deeper, the pain across my chest tightened. Buddy sat with his back to me, cradling Willy. He was muttering and carrying on over Willy's body. I needed to concentrate on the gun on the floor, needed to take it without Buddy knowing that it was missing.

He suddenly scrambled to his feet and stumbled to the back room, careening into scattered cans of icing and an empty grocery cart then he went upstairs. I could hear his feet heavy overhead. He seemed to be searching for something. Furniture was toppled and anything displayed or upright crashed. I seized my opportunity and spread my fingers around Buddy's precious piece. It went into my jacket pocket with Annalise's candles.

I tried to move my legs but couldn't. Something was definitely happening to me. I guessed I could die from untreated shock.

A dark pool of Willy's blood surrounded my body. Willy was gone, Ruby was gone, and Buddy was still wreaking havoc. The radio's pre-dawn broadcast had turned to static, and the TV voiced ghoulish screams from a middle-of-the-night horror flick.

Buddy stomped down the steps and went down either aisle four or five. He seemed to be gathering supplies. He came up the back end of aisle three, but he walked by me without stopping. He had pillows, blankets, and a backpack—Willy's backpack. When Buddy got to the end of our aisle, he dumped the contents of the backpack onto the floor. He stuffed it with jars of pickles, peanut butter and bags of candy. The blankets he pushed in next to the pillows in their cases, and then he pulled a cart out and went down aisle one.

Buddy loaded the wagon with beer, and when he was done went directly to unlock the front door. He was going to take off. His remorse over killing Willy had expired. He started his truck outside the door, its engine loud in the silence. Buddy made several trips to his pick-up. The final one was to bring Diane into the store and lay her next to Willy. Whales Market had become a morgue, a lineup of bodies.

Buddy locked the door and came back to survey aisle three. He had his cell phone and an open beer. He drank four beers before he tried to make a call. His fingers moved awkwardly over the keypad, and he made several attempts at punching numbers without success. He slapped the phone against the side of his head.

"Shit, oh shit," he repeated again and again, punctuating the blows to his head. The alcohol in his system switched a channel in his circuitry and he began to pace back and forth, walking out whatever it was that had managed to get stuck inside him.

Buddy stood over Willy's body. "I'm sorry, man, so fucking sorry." Buddy raised his arms above his head. He twisted and turned like the prop of an airplane and tripped over something. Maybe it was his girlfriend's foot or a triple-pack of prepared vanilla filling; whatever it was, I saw him go down and felt him bounce onto the floor.

He wasn't within my vision, but I could hear him get up onto his knees. As he crawled, the toes of his boots scraped the linoleum. Within a few minutes he came back into my peripheral vision. His long body, in a dog pose, rocked like a ship at sea then buckled onto his side. Buddy brought the cellular phone up close to his face, raised one finger and stabbed at the numbers again. He put the phone on speaker and waited.

Plaintive rings came through from somewhere, from a sleeping house or a too-drunk-to-answer friend. Whoever or wherever Buddy called did not answer. A dry, computerized female voice prompted him to leave a message at the beep. He hung up and tried another number. This time a male voice answered.

"Hey man, I got to come by, turn the light on outside," Buddy said.

"I'm sleeping, man, can't it wait?" the voice asked.

"Fuck no, dude, I'm leaving Whales right now and I'll be at your place in about ten minutes. Just turn the fucking light on and open the door. You can go back to fucking bed after that."

Buddy had walked down aisle three while he was talking. He stopped and stood over me as he instructed his friend on what he needed to do. I opened my eyes and looked straight up into his.

"What the fuck? Goddamn you, Teach." Buddy bent down to get a closer look at me, his cell phone still open, still on speaker, still connected to someone on the outside.

"Nine-one-one!" I screamed. "Whoever you are, call nine-one-one to Whales Market. Buddy's killed Willy and ..." Buddy slammed the phone, dropped it and came down on me. He put one hand over my mouth, and unbuckled his belt with the other.

"I am going to fuck you, Teach. Fuck you like you've never been fucked before, and then break your neck with my bare hands." Buddy fumbled with his jeans. I prayed to Ruby's Lord and closed my fingers around Buddy's gun inside my pocket, then squeezed the trigger.

Buddy's body spasmed as the bullet passed through him. His weight, like Willy's before, settled over me.

Outside the wind howled heralding death's arrival for Buddy. There were no sirens in the distance. If there was a rescue in place it was not imminent. I must have been crazy to think that Buddy's phone friend would call 911. But there was nothing insane about saving myself, nothing foolish about my not wanting to die.

Waiting. Snow fell. More waiting. Buddy's friend must have gone back to bed. I drifted in and out of consciousness. Ruby had told me that the Lord puts you where you are supposed to be. Under Buddy Baker, waiting at Whales for someone to save us, is that what she meant?

Ahh … the sirens, at last, long blasts from their horns like trumpets in the night.

"Friend," Willy had said. I wanted to thank Buddy's friend for not being loyal, for not going back to sleep, for being a friend to me. The sirens were coming to Whales Market. The police would have to run a check on the license plates in the parking lot, my pick-up and Buddy's truck. They probably knew, driving in with lights flashing and sirens blaring in the thickness of morning that something gruesome had happened at Whales.

The rescue vehicles lined up outside the front window and began to suck out the darkness that had enveloped us for hours. The light flooded the store, it roared up and down the aisles exposing Buddy's sins.

They were cautious at first, men afraid of the unknown, of what might lie in wait for them. Watchful faces pushed level against the windows, flattened noses and mouths wreathed in frosted outlines. There was shouting—short, curt commands—then drilling or sawing, whatever was needed to open the front door. All the alarms went off, deafening, reverberating. The first men entered with their guns drawn and cocked. They fanned out in a pre-planned strategy, intent on their mission.

The one who found us was young, *barely big,* the term I used to describe some of my high school students. The snow had compressed his fair hair to his head, and droplets of cold sweat glistened along his cheekbones. Outside, the glare of high beams created a backdrop off his shoulders, an apparition at the end of aisle three. He was armed and held his gun ready to fire but quickly dropped his locked elbow to stand in shock. The child-like face shone in the halo of blinding lights. His brown eyes were pancakes of disbelief. He spoke into a walkie-talkie and soon both ends of aisle three overflowed with helmeted men, an army of saviors.

The EMTs took Buddy's body off mine. They removed the one remaining handcuff between Ruby and me and went to the remains of Willy and Diane. The hum of their monotone voices kept pace with their efforts to salvage any sign of life. I wanted to imagine that mine was not the only heart beating. I wanted to hold out hope for Willy Wu, but I knew his soul had departed. What I did not understand was the lack of attention to me. No one had put their lips to my ear to ask me to squeeze their hand or to move my toes. Someone had checked my pulse, but like Buddy, moved on.

Yellow tape had been erected across the aisles and along the perimeters of Whales Market. Detectives in tan parkas stood silently taking notes. Other, less important personnel spoke in murmurs with eyes that gave away their rank, eyes that shifted into the corners, stealing glances, seeing the horror over and over, but still not comprehending. A few rookies had to turn away. I could hear them retching in the distance.

We were laid out on the floor, feet pointing toward the brownies, heads towards the shortening and oil. Five people; two arms and two legs multiplied became twenty. I could not turn my head. The cold that raged inside of me had dead-bolted my joints. A latex-gloved rescuer passed his fingers across my eyes. Someone else looked at my broken arm and ran their fingers over my blistered lips and burnt tongue, but there was no offer of medication or a splint. My mind was alive, speeding through the mechanics of their labors but unable to send a message, unable to speak.

My physical pain had eased, that I knew, but my recollection is fuzzy at this point. I can't remember the transition to the gurney. It was then that I must have passed out. How long I was unconscious there is no way to know. When I came to, our lineup had been shifted to the space behind the cash register. That is where they pressed me up against the glass and then wheeled the others, one by one, in beside me. Our corner was quiet. The dead do not complain. I was chilled so deep that I felt I had been set in ice, and if I had had my voice, I would have protested.

There was much activity inside the store. Conversations overlapped and were hard to follow. From what I could piece together, there was a body count of five. Five? Buddy, Ruby, Willy, Diane and … Teach! I was dead? The numbers lied. I've been telling this story because Willy saved me, his heroic act could not have been in vain.

"Hey, where are you going?" A thick, hard voice barked at someone coming toward us. "Sir, you are not supposed to be in this area. This is police restricted".

"My wife is here," Jack said.

Jack? Oh, thank the kicked-out saints from heaven, it's Jack. *I'm here Jack. Don't listen to that loser.*

"Your wife is …" The guy hesitated and then went on, "Look, mister, all we got here are dead bodies on gurneys. Are you sure your wife isn't in the ambulance?"

"My wife …" Jack's voice wavered. "One of the detectives sent me over here to identify my wife."

Identify? Oh no, this can't be. No, this isn't right. Have I just been floating around, not ready to cross over? And what about the light, aren't I supposed to see some damn light ... go towards the light ... feel warm and welcome?

"My name is Jack Emerald, my wife's pick-up was in the parking lot. The lieutenant believes my wife was one of the hostages," Jack said. "Can you help me find her? His question floated out into the stillness.

"I'm sorry, Mr. Emerald, I apologize, sir. Yes, of course, I can help you. Do you have some identification, sir? Just a formality." There was a patting of pockets, a wordless exchange and a low murmur of thanks. The wheels on the gurneys gave off small squeaks as each was shifted to make room for the two men.

"I haven't had anyone come through yet, you're the first one, sir." The guy said. "We've got three women, we'll start with this one."

I heard the soft rustle of sheets drawn up and down. There was no response from Jack. Perhaps he just shook his head when he saw Ruby's glazed eye and again when he viewed Diane's shattered face. They were next to me now. The two men blocked the draft from the window and the glare from outside. I didn't realize until that moment that my face was covered. The sheet was pulled away with a soft flutter that tickled my nose.

Jack gasped. He took in such a long breath that I thought *breathe, breathe.*

"Are you all right, Mr. Emerald?" The guy said. "Is this your wife, sir?"

"Yes, this is my wife and, no, I'll never be all right again," Jack said. "Hudson Catalina Emerald, that's her name. Do you need to write that down?"

"Thank you, sir," the guy said. "You can stay with her if you like. It'll be some time before the coroner returns."

"Thanks," Jack said, and he was so close that the word skidded across my face.

"I'll leave you alone, Mr. Emerald," the guy said and moved off, back to guarding the dead.

Jack put his head on my chest against the bulges of candles and pans all clumped together. He was crying. His sorrow penetrated the moisture-proof fabric of my jacket and filled the corner of Whales Market. Jack's mourning came out so profound that it threw a blanket over the cold inside my body. My husband held me in a tight embrace until his tears quieted then he took the cover off and looked at me from head to toe. He stood for a long time with both of his hands wrapped around mine. I felt that he was storing me into a place for retrieval later. Some time in the future, when he needed my hand to hold, Jack would search for this moment and it would be there.

Without a sound, he climbed onto the gurney as if it were our California King. He slipped one arm under my shoulders and the other across my waist. The ridge of his brow pressed against my ear and when he raised his face, his lips brushed my lashes.

"Hudson like the car," he whispered. "Hudson like the car, Catalina like the Island. Hudson Catalina, I love you." He began to cry again. His tears ran down my face and neck. "Oh, Hud," he said. "This can't be right. We must be living someone else's life. You and me, Hud, you and me still have so much to do. I swear your skin feels warm to me, Hud. You can't be dead." He put his fingers to my neck and searched for a pulse. "How am I going to let you go, Hud? You've got to help me."

Jack burrowed into my shoulder, spooning with a corpse. Jack Emerald, I thought, I love you but I don't know how to help. Up until a few minutes ago, I thought I was alive. I believed that Willy Wu had saved my life, and now it seems that his dying has been for nothing. I was looking for a sign, trying to tap into Anna O'Malley for answers, and now you are looking to me to do the same.

"Hudson like the car, Catalina like the Island; Hudson Catalina

I love you." Jack repeated his endearment and I was back at Ten Nettles Cove and the sun was coming up. The snow had stopped and the drifts of white powder shone in the new day's light. Jack kissed me. He kissed my eyes, my nose, my cheeks and my mouth. His lips went down to my neck and found the place, our secret spot that was my cue to speak.

"*Jack ...*"

EPILOGUE

Death comes to everyone. A cemetery becomes home. It is the place that preserves endings and honors lives, long or short.

Folk here on Cape Ann like to say that each town's history is written on its headstones. If that is the case, then what is inscribed there tells us how our ancestors lived, and how they died. More importantly, some enlighten us with a life lesson if we read between the lines. If we pay attention, we learn something.

Ruby Desmond and Willy Wu were *teachers*, the kind of teachers that cross paths and impact lives forever. The two knew that fear and love are the most important of our emotions, love being the elixir for the other. They knew that when fear metastasizes, when fear claims possession of a person's soul, an invitation to bitterness is sent out. An insidious invasion begins as this caustic emotion slowly replaces love.

Willy knew about heroes and Ruby knew about life. In the months and years after the heartbreak at Whales Market, many people on the North Shore knew this fact better than others. Journalists and media swarmed the Cape, pouring money into tourist businesses and taking the peace from her residents. That January blizzard was more like a personal earthquake for the population on the peninsula. Each person was affected by the knowledge that bad things happen not just in big cities with high crime rates, but in their backyards, in their all-night market. Although the Almanac had predicted the storm's coming, it could not have forewarned of the tragedy. There hasn't been a blizzard since, to match that one. The long-time folk, those born and bred on the Cape, will always remember how it was before that night at Whales, how you could go out without locking your door, leave your keys in the car and never worry.

Times and events, like that one at Whales Market, can change everything and change nothing. With the passage of years, the landscape of a yard, a community, a family, a face, a cemetery, and one's perception can be altered, but given enough time, life prefers to return to normal, and memories become everyday wallpaper.

Cape Ann is no exception. Tourists still clog the streets from spring through early fall. Ships come and go in the harbor and for many the tragedy of Whales Market is only a story, a piece of gossip reserved for the curious, tour buses and new neighbors.

Five years have passed since Buddy Baker took three hostages inside Whales Market. The mention of his name stirs up emotions that for the most part are better left quiet.

Buddy was buried next to his mother in New Hampshire. The only inscription on the headstone is the surname: Baker. After his death, the Baker family carried on as usual with indifference, pretty much the way they did when Buddy was alive.

His girlfriend, Diane, had come from the Midwest. She had run away from home at seventeen, and made her way east with money she saved from babysitting. Sometimes Diane thumbed rides rather than pay for a train or bus, and it was on one of these fateful occasions that she met Buddy. They moved in together almost immediately, and that arrangement went on for about six months before Diane found out she was pregnant. Whether Buddy knew about the baby remains an unanswered question. At the time of her death, Diane was eighteen, old enough to vote, to make her own decisions and to answer to life as an adult. Her family came for her remains. They tried to come and go quickly, dodging cameras and nosey reporters. Their intent was to take their daughter home, back to the family plot in a Nebraska cemetery. Mother, father and siblings were devastated by her senseless killing and embarrassed by the publicity surrounding it.

It has taken some time, but those involved have done their best to put that winter night behind them. One of the first orders of public business was to restore Whales Market. Ruby Desmond's Last Will and Testament provided the guidelines for its future. She had requested that the store remain a functioning part of the community, along with keeping the market available to special-needs individuals as a home away from home and a place of employment. Ruby had set up funding for this purpose, and Jeremiah Bothwick's daughters made sure that her wishes were followed, and that the heroism of Willy Wu was honored by renaming the store Willy Wu Market. A group home was created with the remaining property, and it became The Ruby Desmond Home for Lambs of the Lord.

Ruby's body was interred at Ipswich Cemetery in the Desmond family plot. Ipswich was settled largely by Welsh fishermen and prides itself in this fact. The townspeople embraced the opportunity to have Ruby buried in its beloved cemetery. Her stone marker is inscribed: Ruby Jackson Desmond loving wife of Charles Desmond and mother of Abraham Lincoln Desmond, born 1916 died 1999: Alleluia. Abe's flag and medals were buried with her. There isn't a day goes by that Ruby Desmond isn't remembered here on Cape Ann. Willy Wu Market is her legacy, an ever-present reminder of her enduring faith.

Construction on the renovations to the Whales Market property began the first summer after the blizzard. In honor of Ruby, the store never actually closed. There was always at least one aisle open and someone there seven days a week. Willy Wu's two older brothers formed a partnership with the Bothwick sisters and assumed management of the store and residence. It took three years to get the Lambs of the Lord Home up and running with clients and staff. It wasn't until last winter that the market was finished. A special elevator was installed, along with a bathroom for the handicapped and wheelchair ramps going in and out.

Willy Woodrow Wulinsky was buried in Seaside Cemetery in Gloucester. His headstone looks out onto the water. It reads: Willy Wu, loving son and brother, born 1970, died a hero 1999. Friends and family join together once a year at the summer solstice to celebrate his life by rowing across Ipswich Bay. Theoretically, Willy should not have been able to comprehend or reason through the actions required of a heroic deed. To be a hero, a person must put someone else's survival above his own. To save another life could mean the loss of your own: a life for a life. What Willy knew, no one can argue. All the medical jargon written or proposed means nothing in the face of the fact that Willy *did* what was expected of a hero.

Jack Emerald and Victor Catalina are the organizers of the Willy Wu event and see to all the details every year. The Emeralds and the Catalinas were devastated by the losses that night at Whales, so much so that the separation of miles between the families grew intolerable. Claire and Victor sold their home in Sarasota and bought a three-bedroom, clapboard Cape in the town of Annisquam, not far from Ten Nettles Cove. Perhaps Victor always knew the meaning of family, and his role as a father was only skewed in Hudson Catalina's perception. Since the move, both he and Claire have taken up the roles of grandpa and grandma, each giving Annalise and her brothers the good fortune to know them well.

Victor Catalina had long retired from teaching when he returned to Cape Ann, but once back to the place of his childhood, he was able to resolve, and be absolved from, old hurts and resentments. Once freed of these, he took up tutoring high school students, and within a short time he had a steady flow of teenagers, some eager to learn English literature, others guided only by SAT scores.

Claire, a registered nurse by profession, took a position at Ruby's Home for Lambs of the Lord. She became the staff administrator and advisor, a position she filled with wisdom and compassion. Her son, Peter, also relocated to Cape Ann. He bought a small cottage on a side street in Rockport where he set up an art studio. He resigned from his position as a successful graphic designer to pursue the role of mentor to aspiring artists.

Martin Catalina returned to Massachusetts. He had a Masters in Criminal Justice and was a parole officer in the state of Florida. When he moved, Martin was offered a similar job in Fall River. It was here that he reunited with a high school friend, Beth Neves. They married two years ago and moved to Gloucester. Martin, like his father, felt that he had finally come home. He made the decision to turn his hobby—his passion for cooking—into a business, and with Beth's help, they opened a small restaurant near Main Street, just off the wharf. Rose and Joe Catalina would be proud of their grandson and his wife. They have reclaimed the recipes of Catalina's Bistro and incorporated the ambiance of that time into their café. The Emerald children love to go there after school and during summer vacation. Annalise enjoys it most. She has become quite a cook. Together, she and Beth have revived Grandma Rose's clam sauce, lobster bisque, shrimp scampi with risotto and fried calamari.

Martin and Beth's first child will be born this summer, and although Beth remains shy in contrast to her high-strung in-laws and relatives, she blends and balances quite well. Kathy Emerald has taken Beth under her wing, and in doing so has grown quite fond of the girl from Fall River. Unfortunately, the tragedy at Whales Market affected Kathy more than the others. She still carries some measure of responsibility toward what happened, despite knowing that fate was at work and nothing she could have done would have deterred destiny.

Kathy's husband was offered a promotion that would transfer their family to Manchester, New Hampshire. Jack encouraged his sister and brother-in-law to go. He felt that she needed a change of scene, and that perhaps the move would allow some space to build up between her and the past. She and her family left last fall and Cape Ann has not been the same. Her familiar laugh at school events, her passing smiles and half-out-of-the-car waves are still missed. The kids have grown to love the weekends when their cousins come to stay. Ten Nettles Cove buzzes with the sounds of their voices and the smell of favorite foods baking in the oven.

The house at Ten Nettles Cove was painted a pale yellow with green door and shutters, the first spring after the blizzard. Jack Emerald replaced the large oak that split in half during the storm with several small trees. The old oak crushed the roof over the master bedroom during the whiteout, and it was several months before everyone could return to the comfort of Ten Nettles Cove. He kept his office in the house, and works at home more than before. There are two additional employees at the marine laboratory near the harbor, and an ongoing exchange of marine biology grad students who come for the hands-on experience. This arrangement has given Jack more time for the personal research and writing of his oceanographic text book. An offer of a position as a professor at his alma mater in California came in the mail, but he turned it down. Jack said one Emerald leaving Cape Ann was enough for this century.

Yellow Dog passed away three years ago. The family buried his ashes outside Annalise's bedroom window and in Yellow Dog's memory, Jack planted a flower bed of Stargazers. There is no plaque with written words for the dog, just the promise of spring and the blooming of flowers to mark his life.

The oldest Emerald child is a senior at Gloucester High School and the twins will be sophomores in the fall. All the boys are standout basketball players, beans grown from the same stalk as their father. Annalise looks more like her mother everyday. She has the same dark eyes, giant brown buttons set deep in her ten-year-old face.

The past five high school graduating classes made Willy Wu Market their annual fund raising project. Through the students' efforts and energy, a brick path was constructed along the outside perimeter of the Market. The path winds around the store and the home, and down into the parking lot. Each brick holds an inscription written by its donor. Some are anonymous, others have a name or names. The project caught the attention of the media and state officials. Progress was charted on hand-drawn posters, indicating the goal of each class and the next and the next. The parking lot was resurfaced and individual spaces created for shoppers. Cart Return sections are prominent in several locations. Business at the Market has doubled in the past five years. Whales, now Willy Wu's, has become a landmark on the North Shore.

Someone got the bright idea for a ribbon-cutting ceremony to mark the brick walk's completion. A committee was formed consisting of elected town officials, the school board and the high school principal. After much discussion and late-into-the-evening meetings, the committee agreed that the ribbon cutting would be part of this year's commencement. A temporary stage was built to hold the graduates and speakers and rows of folding chairs arranged the length and width of the parking lot.

Many officials were invited, and the Governor of Massachusetts and the Senior Senator of the State were present. The parking lot of what was formerly Whales Market looked like a small stadium. Seats in the first few rows were reserved for the Emerald family, including Kathy, her family and mother. Victor and Claire Catalina were there along with Peter Laskey, Martin Catalina and pregnant Beth. The Wulinskys took up several rows with spouses and children included. Ruby's brother flew up from South Carolina and sat next to Jack Emerald. Seated way in the back, past the parents of graduates and stray onlookers, sat the Goldsteins, Irwin and Carol.

The Willy Wu Market dedication came at the end of commencement, after the diplomas had been handed out and the speeches made about the future. Ruby Desmond would have smiled to hear the Valedictorian say that "life puts you where you are supposed to be all the time." The people in the audience nodded and swished the early summer insects away with their programs. Mr. Romney, the school principal, got up to introduce the Senior Senator. The guests and graduates grew quiet as the Senator, a familiar figure in Massachusetts politics, approached the podium. He began his speech by telling the audience about the memorial plaque that had been installed over the front door of the Market, and with a magician's flourish, he waved his left arm. On cue the sign appeared, and the Senator read the inscription: Willy Woodrow Wulinsky: Friend and Hero.

The microphone squealed. His prepared speech was set aside. The Senator managed to continue briefly, explaining through the disturbance that he was only the opening act, and when the sound system was corrected, the guest speaker would finish up the ceremony and cut the ribbon. His last sentence got caught in a loud shrill that echoed off the folding chairs.

He grimaced. Winnie Olsen, the high school music teacher, bolted onto the stage to fiddle with the equipment. In the thirty or forty seconds that it took to adjust the system, the Senator continued to gesture with his hands like a mime in a three piece suit. He made one last attempt to introduce the guest speaker then returned to his seat. The squealing blocked the audience's applause for the Senator. One long *eeeeeeeee* continued on into a final crescendo and then faded out as the next speaker stepped to the podium.

"My name is Hudson Catalina …"

LINDA MERLINO

I am a writer, and a lined paper junkie. Once upon a time, life kicked me off my writer's path and led me to pursue a more practical profession. Life asked me to hang up my pen, but I couldn't.

As a mother of three children, my most trustworthy partner became a ballpoint. The fiction in my head turned into words on yellow legal pad. I wrote anywhere, any time. No place was my sacred space. I wrote in my car during soccer practices, under an umbrella on rain-drenched sidelines, in fast food restaurants and in chain hotels. I wrote during championship after championship in cities and states, like Jersey, Massapequa, Phoenix, Ithaca, Fayetteville, Staten Island and DC.

Belly of the Whale began in long hand, on the road. The story mushroomed and filled a carton in my back seat amongst soccer balls and tailgate paraphernalia. The kids finally gave me a laptop and I went digital.

I was born in Massachusetts, the setting for *Belly of the Whale*, and home has been New England for most of my adult life. The children have grown and now pursue their own dreams: it is to them that I dedicate my writing.

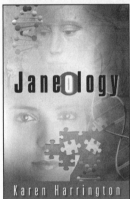

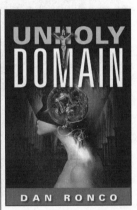

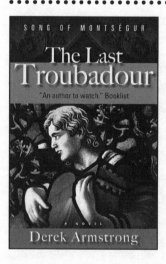
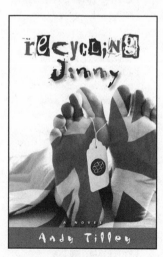

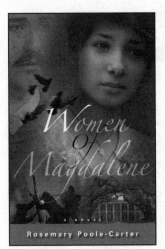

Women Of Magdalene
A hauntingly tragic tale of the old South by Rosemary Poole-Carter

An idealistic young doctor in the post-Civil War South exposes the greed and cruelty at the heart of the Magdalene Ladies' Asylum in this elegant, richly detailed and moving story of love and sacrifice.
- "A fine mix of thriller, historical fiction, and Southern Gothic." *Booklist*
- "A brilliant example of the best historical fiction can do." *ForeWord*

US$ 24.95 | Pages 288, cloth hardcover
ISBN-13: 978-1-60164-014-7
ISBN-10: 1-60164-014-5 | EAN: 9781601640147

On Ice
A road story like no other, by Red Evans

The sudden death of a sad old fiddle player brings new happiness and hope to those who loved him in this charming, earthy, hilarious coming-of-age tale.
- "Evans' humor is broad but infectious ... Evans uses offbeat humor to both entertain and move his readers." *Booklist*

US$ 19.95 | Pages 208, cloth hardcover
ISBN-13: 978-1-60164-015-4
ISBN-10: 1-60164-015-3
EAN: 9781601640154

Truth Or Bare
Offbeat, stylish crime novel by Richard Cahill

The characters throb with vitality, the prose sizzles in this darkly comic page-turner set in the sleazy world of murderous sex workers, the justice system, and the rich who will stop at nothing to get what they want.
- "Cahill has introduced an enticing character ... Let's hope this debut novel isn't the last we hear from him." *Booklist*

US$ 24.95 | Pages 304, cloth hardcover
ISBN-13: 978-1-60164-016-1
ISBN-10: 1-60164-016-1
EAN: 9781601640161

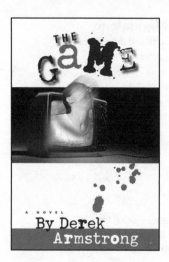

The Game
A thriller by Derek Armstrong

Reality television becomes too real when a killer stalks the cast on America's number one live-broadcast reality show.
■ "A series to watch ... Armstrong injects the trope with new vigor." *Booklist*
US$ 24.95 | Pages 352, cloth hardcover
ISBN 978-1-60164-001-7 | EAN: 9781601640017
LCCN 2006930183

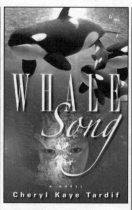

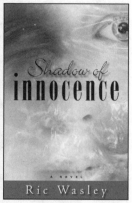

bang BANG
A novel by Lynn Hoffman

In Lynn Hoffman's wickedly funny *bang-BANG*, a waitress crime victim takes on America's obsession with guns and transforms herself in the process. Read along as Paula becomes national hero and villain, enforcer and outlaw, lover and leader. Don't miss Paula Sherman's one-woman quest to change America.
■ "Brilliant"
STARRED REVIEW, *Booklist*
US$ 19.95
Pages 176, cloth hardcover
ISBN 978-1-60164-000-0
EAN 9781601640000
LCCN 2006930182

Whale Song
A novel by Cheryl Kaye Tardif

Whale Song is a haunting tale of change and choice. Cheryl Kaye Tardif's beloved novel—a "wonderful novel that will make a wonderful movie" according to *Writer's Digest*—asks the difficult question, which is the higher morality, love or law?
■ "Crowd-pleasing ... a big hit." *Booklist*
US$ 12.95
Pages 208, UNA trade paper
ISBN 978-1-60164-007-9
EAN 9781601640079
LCCN 2006930188

Shadow of Innocence
A mystery by Ric Wasley

The Thin Man meets *Pulp Fiction* in a unique mystery set amid the drugs-and-music scene of the sixties that touches on all our societal taboos. *Shadow of Innocence* has it all: adventure, sleuthing, drugs, sex, music and a perverse shadowy secret that threatens to tear apart a posh New England town.
US$ 24.95
Pages 304, cloth hardcover
ISBN 978-1-60164-006-2
EAN 9781601640062
LCCN 2006930187

The Secret Ever Keeps
A novel by Art Tirrell

An aging Godfather-like billionaire tycoon regrets a decades-long life of "shady dealings" and seeks reconciliation with a granddaughter who doesn't even know he exists. A sweeping adventure across decades—from Prohibition to today—exploring themes of guilt, greed and forgiveness.
■ "Riveting ... Rhapsodic ... Accomplished." *ForeWord*
US$ 24.95
Pages 352, cloth hardcover
ISBN 978-1-60164-004-8
EAN 9781601640048
LCCN 2006930185

Toonamint of Champions
A wickedly allegorical comedy by Todd Sentell

Todd Sentell pulls out all the stops in his hilarious spoof of the manners and mores of America's most prestigious golf club. A cast of unforgettable characters, speaking a language only a true son of the South could pull off, reveal that behind the gates of fancy private golf clubs lurk some mighty influential freaks.
■ "Bubbly imagination and wacky humor." *ForeWord*
US$ 19.95
Pages 192, cloth hardcover
ISBN 978-1-60164-005-5
EAN 9781601640055
LCCN 2006930186

Mothering Mother
A daughter's humorous and heartbreaking memoir.
Carol D. O'Dell

Mothering Mother is an authentic, "in-the-room" view of a daughter's struggle to care for a dying parent. It will touch you and never leave you.
■ "Beautiful, told with humor... and much love." *Booklist*
■ "I not only loved it, I lived it. I laughed, I smiled and shuddered reading this book." Judith H. Wright, author of over 20 books.
US$ 19.95
Pages 208, cloth hardcover
ISBN 978-1-60164-003-1
EAN 9781601640031
LCCN 2006930184

Rabid
A novel by T K Kenyon

A sexy, savvy, darkly funny tale of ambition, scandal, forbidden love and murder. Nothing is sacred. The graduate student, her professor, his wife, her priest: four brilliantly realized characters spin out of control in a world where science and religion are in constant conflict.
■ "Kenyon is definitely a keeper." STARRED REVIEW, *Booklist*
US$ 26.95 I Pages 480, cloth hardcover
ISBN 978-1-60164-002-4 I EAN: 9781601640024
LCCN 2006930189